Passages

Jo McEntee

Passages

Jo McEntee

ISBN: 978-0-9977051-2-6 (paperback)
ISBN: 978-0-9977051-3-3 (digital)

Library of Congress Control Number: 2017953919

The stories in *Passages* are works of fiction. Names, characters, places and incidents are the products of the author's imagination or are used fictitiously. Any resemblance to actual persons, living or dead, businesses, companies, events or locales is entirely coincidental.

Printed in the United States of America

Dedication

To

Annie Tremont
Eloise Jackson
Isaac Black
Augustus Maxwell
The Williams Family
Robin Patterson
Jordan Christopher
Naomi Banks
Jillian Edwards
David and Evelyn
Nick and Annabelle
Periwinkle Mason
Orabelle Sims
Antoneal Robinson
Daddy Cook
Sugar Crosby
Noah Briggs
Theodora Wells
Sparkle Valentine
Joanna Suarez
Grady and Jasmine Booth

My apologies for not including your stories in this volume. I promise your voices will be heard next time around.

Acknowledgements

To my family and friends, who have graciously and lovingly endured my absence while I forged relationships with my fictional characters. Thank you for all your support and being my village.

To my cohorts at Illinois Humanities, Perspectivists, M-LAS and Writers Workshop. Your critical eyes and ears have pushed me to achieve this milestone.

To my characters, who inspire me, and remind me how they would say or do the things I have them saying and doing. I hope I have done you justice and stayed true to your voice.

To My Beloved Father,

I trust You are well pleased.

Introduction

My tastes are eclectic. I enjoy romances as much as biographies as much as poetry; science fiction and history are equally compelling. And I love speculative endings. Give me a story with an ending that has a little wiggle room to make me wonder, and I'm a hooked fan.

Passages is an eclectic collection of short stories – some funny, some sad, some dark, some romantic. There's murder and sex and kinship and whimsy. Love abounds – in every imaginable form.

When I began writing the short stories in this book, I had no theme in mind. I wrote as I always write – from that place of the familiar sprinkled with a bit of the "what if."

As I read the twenty-four stories as a volume, it was obvious that the characters in each story were moving – passing, as it were – from one place to another. I drew my title from this. Sometimes the passage is through physical dimensions; sometimes, it is a philosophical mindset that evolves. On occasion, it's both.

What was not immediately obvious was how the passages taken or not taken affected each character's internal and external world, profoundly defining beginnings *and* endings in a single step. Or misstep. And happily, ever after is … well… you'll see. Sometimes all you need is something different.

Enjoy.

Stories

Stories (continued)

Stories (continued)

When hurt overwhelms
Sometimes the only solace
Is to hurt right back

Petite Soeur

I haven't flown a kite since the summer I was nine years old. That summer was the first time I killed. I was lousy at kite flying – still am, for that matter. I excel at killing, though. I revel in the planning and execution. And any remorse is abated by the necessity of the circumstance.

~=~=~=~=~=~=~=~

I picture myself that summer day, 18 years ago, standing in knee-deep weeds struggling to keep an old box kite airborne for more than a minute. It was this simple act that attracted the attention of Sonny Wells.

Twenty-two-year-old Sony was well known in Ridgely as a womanizing jock, albeit a charming one. His popularity and fan base had waned in recent months with the accusation of raping fifteen-year-old Mary Jessup. His entourage of wannabes and worshipers had disappeared. He was a pariah, alone and kind of sad in a way.

"Hey little man," Sonny called out as he approached me. "Let me show you how to get it up and keep it up."

I had been too young at the time to understand the innuendo, but the fact that Sonny said this while adjusting his private parts seemed very wrong and insulting. Even more insulting was that he thought I was a boy. True, my pigtails were hidden under a baseball cap, and I wore dungarees, a T-shirt and Converse high-tops. But how else would I dress to fly a kite? Or kill a bad man? Regardless, Sonny should have known I was a girl.

His insults on top of the injury to Mary strengthened my resolve to cull Sonny Wells from the predators. Of course, at the time, my thought process was not that sophisticated. All I knew was that my cousin Mary, who was like a big sister to me, screamed herself awake every night after Sonny raped her.

At nine, I wasn't even sure I understood what rape meant. The dictionary definitions were about robbing and despoiling and taking away by force. Whatever Sonny had taken away, it was horrible enough to cause Mary to cling to her pillow and not talk to me. I was determined to make Sonny Wells pay for what he'd done, since no one else seemed up to the task.

Sonny had shown a childlike fascination in flying that kite. He was almost likeable that day. It was too little, too late. My decision was final. When the kite landed in a thick patch of weeds on the eastern border of the grove, Sonny went to fetch it. I fetched Grandpa's Ruger I had hidden among the ragweed and cocklebur, eased up within a yard behind Sonny, and standing my ground, steadied my gun hand with my right hand and squeezed the trigger. The bullet hit Sonny at the base of his neck, severing his spinal cord. It was the kill shot Grandpa had shown me to take down bear.

When Grandpa figured out it was I who killed Sonny Wells he took every measure to protect me. Not that anyone cared. Neither the police nor Sonny's cronies mourned his passing. Sonny had alienated so many people and burned so many bridges by then that the list of suspects resembled the neighborhood white pages. Some even bragged on the sly that he (or she) was the one who had laid Sonny to rest.

Grandpa knew. He sent me to live with Great-Aunt Myrtle, his sister in Devereux Heights. I never could shake the feeling that Grandpa was tormented by what I had done. We never were the same after that. He would visit me each month, but it was always perfunctory. He made sure I had enough of everything: food, clothes, schooling, money, but we were never the same after Sonny. We didn't go hunting or fishing. We no longer sat on the porch in the evenings, counting cricket chirps and predicting the weather.

~=~=~=~=~=~=~

Now, here at Grandpa's grave, the bigger part of me longs for that carefree relationship we had. I hadn't been able to come home for his funeral, and part of me was glad that my work kept me away. I know my deeds were wicked and caused him much grief. I make no apologies. I did what I needed to do.

The kite I am flying today tugs on the line. I let out a couple more meters of cord and watch the diamond-shaped kite climb above the treetops, its tail bobbing merrily as it soars toward the clouds and rising sun. I kneel by the headstone and trace the carved lettering with my fingertips:

Joshua Francis Lewis
Loving Husband, Father, Brother, Friend
24 April 1937 - 19 August 2015

No mention of grandchildren. I guess Mary and I aren't part of the memories anyone wants to preserve.

I cut the line and watch the kite disappear into the sky. I leave the cemetery. I have one more piece of family business to take care of before I go back to my life.

~=~=~=~=~=~=~

Exactly fifty-two minutes later I drive the rented Renegade into the thick brush behind the squalid camper parked in the clearing near the bluff. This is the place that Mary Jessup calls home these days.

"You sure can pick 'em, Cousin." This one, Beau Richards, has the nasty habit of beating Mary, then passing her around to his friends.

~=~=~=~=~=~=~

Twice before, Mary had chosen unwisely. The first time was two months into her high school senior year. Mary dropped out of high school to live happily ever after with Mitchell Warren. He was fifteen years older and had four incorrigible kids – ages 12, 9, 7 and 4 – desperately in need of a mother. I always suspected that the mother died by her own hand to get away from her husband and those brats.

Not before long Mary was pregnant. Hers was a difficult pregnancy, and neither Mitchell nor his offspring lifted a finger to help around the house.

One Wednesday, while the family was out for their weekly movie night, Mary lost the baby and nearly her own life. Carrying a basket load of laundry downstairs, she slipped on a miniature race car and crashed full-force onto the concrete slab basement floor. She lay there for hours bleeding.

Gossipy Miss Evie Washington, who volunteered at the hospital, told Grandpa who told Aunt Myrtle that when Mitchell Warren brought Mary into the hospital, he was not the least bit concerned about the baby he and Mary had lost, or that Mary would never have a child of her own. His primary concern was his children. He berated Mary for her carelessness: who would take care of his children while she lazed in this expensive hospital room?

By the time Mary was ready to leave the hospital, two things had happened. I had made the three-mile trip between Deveraux Heights and Ridgely twice without anyone missing me, and Mitchell Warren and his children died from botulism — most certainly from the home-canned tomato soup they had eaten.

After the sudden deaths of the Warren family, Grandpa and Aunt Myrtle thought it best to send me to St. Clotilde Catholic Boarding School for Girls in California. They felt it best to put a greater distance between me and Mary.

~=~=~=~=~=~=~

I survey the area before approaching the camper. It's angled awkwardly among the white oak, its left front wheel obscured by a clump of spicebush. At the rear of the camper, I hoist myself up to peak through the window. A shadeless lamp illuminates the bedroom. On the bed Mary lays in a quasi-fetal position, her lower arm encased in a stained plaster cast. Her face is bruised and swollen. She looks like she's gone several rounds with an opponent way above her weight class, and lost. Beau is passed out between the bed and the wall, his arm still tied off with a makeshift tourniquet, the needle dangling from his collapsed vein.

I tap on the window. Neither of them move. I drop to the ground and circle the trailer. No one notices as I draw the .357 magnum from its shoulder holster and enter the trailer. I walk back to the bedroom. Beau is still out for the count. Too bad this will be painless for him.

I stand over Mary and watch her labored breaths. No doubt her ribs have taken a pummeling as well as her face. There are several prescription bottles lined up on the nightstand and a half-empty half-pint of whiskey. Sobriety is not a common theme in Mary's life of late.

~=~=~=~=~=~=~

Six years ago, it looked like Mary's life was turning around. She moved to Springfield and completed an office technology course. She got a job as an administrative assistant at a boutique investment firm, and began dating one of the junior partners, Riley Hawthorne. Things began to look up for Mary. She developed a becoming self-assured sophistication. In her letters to me she started calling me "petite soeur" – little sister. I liked that.

Riley introduced Mary to fine art, five-star dining and charity benefits. He also introduced her to cocaine and ketamine. Mary was so enraptured by the ck that within a year she had lost both the job and Riley. But she clung to the ck, doing whatever was necessary to maintain that relationship. Grandpa eventually got her in a rehab facility. Actually, a couple of times. Mary was never completely clean and sober for long.

Poor Riley was not so lucky. He got hold of a nasty batch of ck and it killed him. He really shouldn't have bought drugs from a stranger.

~=~=~=~=~=~=~

I wonder why the men in Mary's life enabled her pain. Couldn't they see the damage they did? Didn't they care?

I sit down on the bed, laying the gun between us. I smooth the matted hair away from her ear. "I love you, Mary," I whisper.

No one will ever understand the complexity of the bond I have with Mary. Even I am unable to explain it. I have searched my soul, and still have no clue as to why I am tethered to Mary in such a steadfast way. I do not know why her pain affects me so. Only God knows what compels me to hurt those who hurt her.

I take the syringe filled with suxamethonium chloride from the concealed pocket of my jacket. I look at Mary's arms. None of the needle marks is fresh enough to reuse.

I lovingly place my hand on Mary's cheek and insert the needle into her ear, angling it until it touches the tympanic membrane. My hand steadies Mary's face as I drive the needle into the depths of her middle ear and push the plunger.

Mary's eyes open as I extract the needle. I see the confusion as she tries to focus. She smiles at me and tries to get up. But her smile fades and her limbs fail. Her eyes remain open; she sees into me. Slowly, the drug steals her labored breaths. Six minutes. Her heart is still.

~=~=~=~=~=~=~=~

The summer before Sonny, Grandpa and I spent many early mornings on Lake Springfield. On one occasion he said to me, "Well, Baby Girl, it's time to decide, fish or cut bait?"

"What do you mean Grandpa?"

"Sometimes, like now, when we been fishing all morning, and the fish just keep nibbling away at the bait, but not biting the hook, you've got to decide if you're going to keep fishing or call it a day."

"But it's not good to give up. Right Grandpa?"

"Baby Girl, sometimes you have to give up – cut bait – in order to fully commit to another day and another task. There's no shame in starting over, if you've given it your all."

~=~=~=~=~=~=~

I remember this as I place the syringe back in its secret place. I holster the gun and wipe the stinging tears from my eyes. As I reach the bedroom door, Beau stirs. Forgetful me, I almost neglected dear Beau. I draw and aim. One shot to the head. Now I can forget him.

~=~=~=~=~=~=~

Two hours later, I have deposited the .357 in a drainage ditch and dropped off the rental car.

"Sister Mary Francis!" Johnny Robinson and several other fourth graders run to greet me as I enter the Springfield train station. "We thought you'd miss the train to Chicago."

"That would be tragic," Sharon Owens shrieks.

"Settle down," Sister Bernice says to the children. She turns to me and asks, "Did you find peace and closure with your family?"

"Yes," I reply. "Thank you for allowing me to make the trip to Ridgely. It felt good to sit by my Grandpa's grave and reminisce. I put things in order. I did what I needed to do."

Sister Bernice smiles at me. "Let's get the children on board. We have quite an adventure ahead of us."

"Yes. We do," I agree. I am fully focused on the task at hand. "Chicago, here we come!" I cheer, leading the children out to the platform to board the train.

A difficult choice
To be brave and not settle
First, let go of fear

360

Had it been just a bit darker and the light on the footpath a bit dimmer, Elmer Patterson would not have noticed it. Had it been anything else lying in the runoff water surrounding the drinking fountain, Elmer would have passed it by.

His love of books compelled him to bend down and rescue the leather-bound journal from the muddy puddle that threatened to be its demise. As Elmer picked up the journal, wrapped it in his clean white handkerchief and placed it in his jacket pocket, he had no other intention than to preserve it. He gave no thought to its contents or the repercussions of this action.

Five blocks and as many minutes later, alone in his renovated condominium apartment, Elmer took the journal from his pocket and examined it. It was leather, not an imitation, and hand stitched as well. Its edges were gilded, its pages stuck together, its ink spreading in Rorschach-like patterns.

Elmer brought the roll of paper towels from the under-cabinet holder and placed it on the island table. He pulled out a stool and sat, then began to meticulously separate each page from its adjacent leaf, placing a section of paper towel between them. When he had finished, the journal was nearly tripled in bulk and resembled an accordion's fanned bellows.

Elmer walked to the adjacent dining area and looked at the timepiece nestled among hundreds of books in the artisan bookcase. It was well after his accustomed bedtime. He tidied up, performed his post-evening walk rituals, and went to bed.

~=~=~=~=~=~=~

The next morning when he woke, Elmer's first thought was of the journal. He wondered who it belonged to – if the owner realized the loss. He imagined the owner desperately searching for it. After all, such a handsomely crafted journal must hold significant meaning.

Elmer went to the kitchen to inspect the results of his work from the night before. The pages had dried, and he removed the paper towels from between them. He turned to the first page, looking for marks of ownership. There were none. He closed the journal, started the coffee maker, and headed to the shower.

~=~=~=~=~=~=~

Fresh from his shower and dressed for a leisurely Saturday of reading, Elmer filled his mug with coffee and took it out onto the terrace. The view was not spectacular, but it did offer a relaxing venue to devour coffee, chocolate croissants and a novel.

Elmer tried to concentrate on the novel, but his mind kept drifting back to the journal. He returned to the kitchen and thumbed through the warped pages. The writing was too smeared to fully decipher, but he gathered its author was a woman. There were intimate details of failed love affairs and dashed dreams. The bits and pieces he read made him feel at once empathetic and intrusive.

And then he came to a page, clearly dated and legible. It was written just three days ago. He read the passage twice before he could bring himself to acknowledge its meaning.

> *I am 39 years old. It is time to end this life I have come to abhor. I am tired of mistakes, recriminations and false starts. I have had enough! Saturday at two o'clock, at the 360 Observation Deck, it ends. So long, Donna Tucker, it's been a slice!*

Elmer looked at his watch; it was 12:18. What should he do?

Four years ago, when he was standing on the precipice of 40, he had taken similar stock of his life. The conclusion: he and his life were boring. He had friends, but most were happily coupled. He had worked for the same accounting firm for twenty years, moving up from summer intern to senior management. His was an uneventful life. No wonder there was no one anxious to share in it. Even among his bibliophile peers he was an oddity. His tastes were eclectic: he consumed fiction and non-fiction with equal voracity. A friend had joked, "Elmer would delight in reading a cereal box." How boring!

Elmer had not been in a serious relationship at the time, and his melancholia had lasted for months. When he finally emerged from it, he was armed with the realization that when "it" happened – whatever "it" was – he would be ready.

This was what he wanted to tell Donna Tucker. Not to give up, that there was always hope that "it" would happen. But you must be "here" to receive "it."

How could he tell her? He needed a plan. He knew where she would be at two o'clock. He would go there now, look for someone with despair in their eyes, and tell her not to quit life. Not the greatest of plans, but it was all he had.

Out on the street, Elmer hailed a taxi and headed downtown to 360.

~=~=~=~=~=~=~

Elmer had not anticipated the long line of natives and tourists eager to see the 360-degree cityscape from ninety-four floors above. As the line inched along and the time ticked away, Elmer panicked that he might be too late.

Finally, ticket in hand, he boarded the elevator to the observation deck. When the doors opened he could hear cathedral bells chiming the hour. Frantically he searched the faces to his left and to his right, then in a burst of uncharacteristically manic energy he shouted, "DONNA. DONNA TUCKER. DON'T THROW YOUR LIFE AWAY."

All eyes were riveted on him.

And then a man kneeling on one knee in front of a lovely brunette rose and asked, "Who is this guy?"

"I don't know," the brunette responded. Elmer Patterson moved to stand beside the woman who must be Donna Tucker. She turned to Elmer and asked, "Who are you?"

"My name is Elmer Patterson. I found your journal in the park." Elmer rattled on, profusely apologizing for reading her private thoughts, and for committing this enormous faux pas. In all honesty, he had thought her last entry was a suicide note.

And it was at that moment, while listening to this bespectacled, unassuming man, that Donna Tucker saw an unobstructed view of her life. Thank the gods for this reality check! She was about to succumb to biological clocks and family pressure and accept a marriage proposal for all the wrong reasons, rather than wait and marry for love, or not marry at all. Suddenly she felt very brave and empowered once more.

Donna turned to her would-be fiancé and said, "No."

"No," the man echoed, disbelieving.

"No," Donna repeated.

Politely, Elmer offered Donna his arm, which she hesitantly took. Both smiled self-consciously as the crowd that had surrounded them – to get a better glimpse of the drama – parted to let them through.

~=~=~=~=~=~=~

Down on the street, Elmer handed the journal to Donna.

"You read my journal," she deadpanned. "I may have to kill you."

"Would you like to get something to eat instead?" Elmer asked.

Donna looked at the water-stained leather and plumped pages. "Yes," she said, "I'd like that."

"You know this may not be 'happily ever after'," Elmer said.

"I know," Donna replied, "and it's perfectly alright."

Magical moonlight
Perhaps a chance encounter
Tonight, we are one

Just for Tonight

She had walked into the hotel lounge with the self-assurance of a woman who did not need the validation of others to define herself. Impeccably groomed, she was tall – five-foot-nine – her sexy strappy heels bringing her height to six feet. He still had a couple of inches on her, though. Her dark auburn hair was pulled back into a loose ponytail held by ebony combs. She wore a classic black wrap dress that skimmed her shapely body, stopping several inches above her knees. A diamond tennis choker adorned her neck, a matching bracelet on her wrist. She wore no rings or bands on her left hand. The tiny clutch she carried couldn't possibly hold more than a lipstick and credit card. Maybe a condom if he were lucky.

Instantly he ached to experience whatever this woman had to offer.

From across the room, he watched her talk with a couple. He started to move through the crowd, towards this mesmerizing woman, when he saw a man slip an arm around her waist and present her with an affectionate kiss on her cheek. He hated this man, whoever he was. She bestowed on the mystery man a smile that exuded warmth and sensuality. That smile aroused him clear across the room. Another man joined them, introductions were made, and their body language clearly confirmed that the two men were a couple.

He didn't care who these people were or what they meant to her. If they were the gauntlet he had to maneuver to access her, they were as good as gone. Undaunted, he continued his approach, his single intent to rescue this woman from fifth wheel status and have her all to himself. Standing before the group, he gave them a token nod while extending his hand to her. She took it, ignoring the curious glances of her companions. Their touch generated audible sparks.

An instrumental version of *At Last* wafted through the space. On the dance floor, he molded her body to his. They were a perfect fit. Every inch of her radiated a hunger he was eager to satisfy. There was no need to ply this woman with alcohol, nor seduce her with witty conversation. Their mutual lust was intoxicating and seductive enough. He drank in her scent and imagined what she was wearing beneath her dress. *Something black. Or maybe red?* The very thought hardened him. She looked up into his eyes – acknowledging, approving his brand of appreciation.

When the music stopped, their melded bodies screamed for more. Slowly they separated. She opened her purse, took out a room key card and discreetly slipped it into his jacket pocket. She tossed him a pouty smile, turned and walked out of the lounge.

The sway of her hips beckoned him to follow. And he did. He caught up to her at the elevator, which they entered with other hotel guests. They stood side by side, their fingertips barely touching. Desire flowed dizzily between them. He was in an erotic stupor when he followed her off the elevator at the twelfth floor.

At the end of the hall they entered a room illuminated by cityscape lights. Before he closed the door, she slipped the *Do Not*

Disturb sign on the door handle. She further emphasized her desire for uninterrupted seclusion by sliding the chain lock into its track.

She moved in front of him, slipping her hands under the front of his jacket, easing it off his shoulders, letting it drop to the floor. He left it were it fell as he watched her sashay further into the room, stepping out of her shoes as she did. She removed the combs from her hair and fluffed the loose mane. His dick rose to attention again.

He stepped to her, wrapping his arms around her, pressing his erection into her backside. He kissed her neck and felt the charge travel through her body. She leaned into him, slowly turning to face him. The friction fueled the fire in his groin. She tilted her face up and offered her sensuous mouth for his exploration.

He buried his tongue deep in her mouth. He tasted ginger and honey. *What had she been eating?* When he came up for air he noticed that she had managed to unbutton his shirt and loosen his belt. He was losing all sense of time with this woman, and he didn't want it any other way.

Again, he wondered what lay beneath the dress. He unwrapped her like the gift she was. He was totally enchanted. She was wearing white - lacy, tiny and sheer. It suited her. He quickly shed shirt, shoes, slacks and socks. She smiled a temptress' smile as she eyed the huge bulge in his black jersey briefs.

Her hand slid beneath the fabric. Her fingers expertly traced the throbbing vein that was soon to be his undoing. He took her hand away and led her to a spot in the room bathed in moonlight. He circled her, absorbing her essence, stopping only to remove her scant undergarments. He kissed her again, pleased to feel her breathing matched the erratic beating of his own heart.

He continued to circle her, taking in every lush curve. His fingertips lingered over delicious bits of her body: her delicate earlobes, the valley between her full breasts, her protruding nipples, the hemispheres of her derrière, the titillating crook of her knee. He knelt before her, kissing the hint of roundness at her tummy, gently sucking at the concave of her belly button. He purposefully planted wet kisses on her inner thighs, just as purposefully avoiding the place between them where they each craved his mouth to be. When she literally could not stand any longer under the onslaught of his caresses, he carried her to bed.

He took off his briefs and crawled between her legs. Eight-and-a-half inches of rock hard dick enthusiastically greeted her. He brought the slick swollen tip to her gate, her heat sending his growing balls into a frenzied mating dance. Pure. Ecstasy. They still did not speak. Only their shared sighs and moans breached the silence, their fiery heat encased in a magical muteness.

She placed her hands firmly on his shoulders and pushed him off her and onto his back. She reached under the pillow and withdrew a condom. Sensually she unwrapped it, placed it in her mouth and proceeded to slowly sheath him. Her mouth and tongue threatened to exhaust him. It was the most erotic blow job he had ever experienced. She stopped abruptly. Raising an eyebrow, she challenged him to make the next move.

He flipped her onto her back and pinned her beneath him. Passionate kisses muffled their wanton cries. He entered her slowly, possessively, the walls of her hot wet passageway closing in around him, then opening ever so slightly as he pushed onward. Closing. Opening. Inch by inch he eased down the slippery path until he banged his head into a dead end. He retreated, then advanced. Retreated. Advanced. She arched her back and wrapped her long luscious legs around his waist, thwarting his retreats. He reconciled himself to an unconditional surrender as her pulsating walls ripped the orgasms from them both.

~=~=~=~=~=~

He awoke to an empty bed, the scent of them still lingering in the air. He searched the darkness and saw her naked silhouette. She was going through his pockets – first his pants, then his suit jacket.

He was off the bed and beside her in an instant. She did not flinch when his hand encircled her wrist. She met his eyes, before her gaze fell on the iPhone he held in his other hand.

"Is this what you're looking for?" These words were the first spoken between them since meeting in the lounge.

She nodded.

He led her to the plush club chair, sat and pulled her onto his lap. He applied his thumbprint to the home button, then swiped to an app where he entered a sequence of numbers. He held the screen so that they both had a clear view of the image.

Across town in her crib, their beautifully perfect, perfectly beautiful six-week-old daughter slept peacefully. He scanned the other rooms of the house and found the infant's two grandmothers in the kitchen playing cards, a baby monitor sitting on the table between them.

"Did I spoil your fantasy?" she asked.

"No, never." He covered her mouth with kisses. "Never," he repeated. "You *are* my fantasy. The only fantasy I'll ever need."

He thought to break their agreed upon vow of silence with one last question of his own. "About that condom trick..."

She whispered in his ear, "YouTube. I perfected my technique with a banana." The warmth of her breath shivered him to his core.

Lucky banana. His grin was broad. *Luckier me. God, I loved this woman! My woman! My wife!*

He scooped her up and carried her back to bed, taking the cell phone from her and laying it on the nightstand charging pad. He then turned his attention to her most sensitive button, silently vowing to push it again and again until they were both deliriously sated.

That which we hold dear
Is often more frightening
Than letting it go

Percy's Den

Percy's Den is the kind of establishment where everyone knows your name and keeps it to themselves. I hadn't been here in over a year, but I still got the brotherly nods as I climbed onto my stool. Percy Longfellow, owner and bartender, placed my usual Jack and Coke in front of me as I surveyed the joint. I inhaled deeply, sniffing out the newbies and interlopers. It would be entertaining tonight.

I watched a trio of frat boys in the back alcove playing pool. It was not uncommon for outsiders to turn up here: a wrong turn and you're riding around in circles on the backroads. Dimly lit as it was, Percy's was a beckoning oasis to the lost traveler.

The two boys at the table were drunk and loud, each trying to out-alpha-male the other. The third boy was quiet – he radiated a sadness that he chose not to drown in booze. I heard him approach the bar and stand beside me.

"I'll have another," he said to Percy, pointing at his empty glass.

"You should add some Jack to that Coke," I said, raising my glass to him.

"Can't tonight. I'm the designated driver."

"No fun in that," I observed.

"I'm not much in the fun mood."

"Woman problems," I said.

"How'd you guess?"

"I could hear your broken heart across the room." *And I can smell her scent on you. How long had it been since they'd been together? Scratch that thought. I didn't want to know. I preferred to believe she had innocently worn that shirt he was wearing.*

"I guess I could be a bit cooler about it – if it shows that much," he said, breaking into my thoughts.

"Why? If you love her, don't hide it. Especially from her." I'm great at giving advice; not so good at following it. That's my nature.

"Bruce Wilson," he said taking the stool next to me.

"Nick," I said. "Nick Keams." The regulars' ears perked up as we exchanged names. I smiled. "So, what brings you to Percy's Den? We're a bit off the main thoroughfare."

"My buddies thought I needed to get out and get laid. We were headed over to Tastee's, but somehow ended up here. Just as well…," he shrugged.

"So, tell me about the girl," I said.

"What's to say? She and I are from different worlds. According to her."

"Really? Which planet is she from? I'm just assuming you're the earthling. You are, aren't you?"

Bruce eyed me suspiciously. "How many of those have you had?" he asked indicating my glass, which Percy was refilling.

"On my way to enough," I replied. "Look, I've been where you're sitting. In fact, I met a girl from around here and fell hard – real hard. Pretty much the way you're feeling now."

I could feel the eyes burrowing into me. The regulars were none too keen about my waxing nostalgic with this boy.

"Let's take this out back," I suggested. "Too many prying eyes and big ears."

Bruce glanced over his shoulder at his buddies – still engaged in their one-upmanship battle. "Heading out back," he yelled to the pair. Neither responded.

I reached over the bar and got my bottle of Jack and a couple cans of Coke before slipping out the door. Drinks in tow, we headed for the beaten down grass parking lot behind Percy's Den. I sauntered over to my shiny jet black pimped-out '56 F100 and leaned against the fender.

Bruce stopped to admire the truck before following suit. *Points to the boy for that.*

"Tell me about your girl," I prompted.

"You first," Bruce countered.

Never one to pass up an opportunity to talk about myself, I launched into my tale. "Her name was Annabelle. From the moment I met her, I knew I would die for her. It was that strong. That was seventeen – no eighteen – years ago. Love of my life. She died a year ago. Hunting accident."

"Sorry," Bruce said. "Any kids?"

"Just one. A daughter, almost eighteen. Smart as a whip. Working towards a zoology degree. Kid idolizes Dave Mech."

I watched his expression as he put the pieces together. "You're Theda's dad," Bruce accused.

"Guilty," I said.

The boy was quick – I felt the blow before I saw it coming. Maybe the drink was slowing me down.

"How could you abandon Theda like that? She needed you."

"Watch your mouth, Pup. You don't know what you're talking about."

I sprang to my feet, rubbing my jaw. My face was a few inches from Bruce's. My lip curled and my eyes glowed amber, then red, and amber again. It was Bruce's turn to hit the ground. *Points to me.*

"What the fuck..."

"Watch your mouth, Pup," I warned again.

The music from inside was louder now, pulsating in the still night air. *The games must've begun.*

Bruce back-scooted away from me on his ass. I closed the distance between us and dragged him up with one swift jerk. I held him in the air, his feet flailing several inches off the ground – just to hammer home my point. The shock in his eyes was tempered only slightly by his curiosity. I put Bruce down carefully, and mock dusted him off.

Bruce brushed my hand away. "I don't know you Nick. I don't care who you are or how tough you are. I know you were a lousy father to Theda when she needed you most. She deserved better. She deserves better."

Damn! He was like a dog with a bone. He was not about to let my sorry-ass parenting skills slide. *Again, points go to the Pup.*

"You've never loved a woman the way I loved Annabelle. From the first moment – it was like we had found our missing pieces in each other. When she died, I couldn't function. I was lost. I didn't want to live."

"Which makes you a selfish bastard, Nick. You should have wanted to live for Theda. She's your and Annabelle's daughter."

"Now hold on a minute…"

"No, Nick. You hold on. You're going to listen to me. Do you have any idea the trauma Theda's come through?"

"I think I do. More so than you. But you tell me. Go on, Pup." I leaned back on the Ford. *This boy has nerve.*

"When I first saw Theda, she was just going through the motions. She had lost both her parents: her mother was killed in a hunting accident; her grieving father had taken off. She had my heart from the very first. And it wasn't pity. And it wasn't her needing me. It just felt so right when we were together. We just started hanging out – eating together, doing our homework, studying. We'd go for runs through the woods. We thrived on being together. And it isn't about the sex, although…"

"OK. We can skip that part. What broke you up? Cheat on her?"

"God no! I can't think of another girl since Theda. I don't know what I did." The sadness in Bruce's voice invaded my senses. Maybe he did know the kind of love I shared with Annabelle.

"Theda is her mother's daughter," I told Bruce. "My guess is she bolted because you were talking marriage and commitment."

A scream cried out over the music, assaulting our space. Bruce jumped, hesitating only a moment before heading towards the bar. I blocked his path to the Den.

"You don't want to go in there," I said.

"My friends are in there. That sounded like Blake."

"How old are you, Pup?"

"Nineteen – twenty next week. What's that got to do with anything? And stop calling me Pup."

Bruce tried to sidestep me, but I continued to block his path. He froze as the screams were replaced with guttural growls and the sounds of ripping flesh.

"You love Theda." I needn't have asked; I could smell it.

"Yes. With all my heart."

Right answer. "Stand behind me – and stay there. That's if you want to see my daughter again. And that next birthday."

A huge grey wolf, its muzzle covered in fresh blood stood in the doorway. In less than a minute it morphed into Percy. His brother,

Thad, joined him. Ever the showboater, Thad – already in human form – was gnawing on a hand formerly attached to one of the frat boys. He spat out a class ring, which landed in full view of Bruce, who promptly tossed his last meal and then some.

"Allow me to introduce Theda's uncles." Bruce was too busy dry heaving to look up.

"Kid's a problem, Nick. Take care of him or we will," Percy advised.

"Your choice, Pup," I said to Bruce – never taking my eyes off the Longfellows. "Them or me?"

"I choose Theda. Always."

Right answer.

I turned.

Bruce stood his ground as I buried my teeth in his throat.

~=~=~=~=~=~

Six Months Later

"To love and family," Percy toasted.

"Love and family," everyone echoed.

"It's a thing of beauty," Thad slobbered.

I waited until all the congratulatory speeches and backslapping subsided before rescuing my future son-in-law from the Den. We went out back – Jack and Coke in tow – as we have done many times since that first night.

"Last night of freedom," I said, passing the bottle to Bruce. He took a healthy swig and passed it back. He popped the tab on the can and let the cola chase down the mash.

"Doesn't feel that way."

"You're suited to this life. Some are born into it like the Longfellows. Others, like you and me, choose it. For love."

As if on cue, Bruce got that glazed-over puppy dog look in his eyes. Theda was near.

"Uh, Nick, the party's been great. Make my apologies, will you? I got to run."

I watched Bruce transform into a muscular brown wolf, sprinting to the clearing where the sleek tan-tipped female waited. Together they set off at a playful canter, nipping at each other as they disappeared into the woods.

Sin of my parents
Self-sentenced solitude
Until self saw me

Because I've Learned to Love Kitty DiMarco

"It was a mistake coming here," Alex said to Kitty in his beautifully Italian-accented English. They had just returned from the hospital to their room at Delia's B & B.

Kitty smiled tentatively at her husband. He was right, and in the back of her mind she had known that no good would come from seeing her mother. Still, she had wanted to try.

She had not wanted to believe that her mother, frail and weak on her death bed, would still hold Kitty responsible for the sins of her father. But she did – Lilly Mae Rodgers held on to her hatred and bitterness until her last breath.

After a week of sitting by her mother's bedside, praying for a miracle, praying for Lilly Mae to rally and speak all the words of love and regret Kitty had longed to hear from her all her life, Lilly Mae declared in a raspy voice, "I want to look at you one last time and curse your life for ruining mine." She had tried to spit in Kitty's face, but only managed to drool pathetically from the side of her mouth.

Twenty minutes later, Lilly Mae Rodgers, her body shriveled by cancer, died.

Now, Alex put his arms around Kitty. He didn't know how to comfort her grief. He had not been a part of Kitty's life when her Gramma Jean died. She had shouldered that burden with Mama Sissy's help. And when Kitty had lost Mama Sissy, he had known what to say and do. "Remember all the things you shared," he told her as they looked through hundreds of photos taken over the years, looking for just the right one to grace the funeral program.

But how do you comfort someone whose only memories are painful? In all of Kitty's life there was not a single memory between mother and daughter that spoke of love and kinship. Kitty's was an incomprehensible loss.

Kitty extracted herself from Alex's embrace. "I just need some time alone," she told him. Kitty went into the bedroom and shut the door, leaving Alex standing in the sitting room.

~=~=~=~=~=~

It was well into the evening when Kitty emerged from the bedroom. Alex, who had stretched out on the chintz-covered couch in the sitting room, bolted upright at the sound of the bedroom door opening. Kitty reached him before he stood. She sat down next to him and handed him an envelope.

"I love you."

Alex smiled. He never tired of hearing this. He put his arm around her, drew her closer, and kissed her forehead.

"Ti amo," Alex replied.

He removed the pale ivory sheets from the envelope, unfolded them and began reading Kitty's graceful cursive handwriting.

Dear Mother,

I have always thought of you as my mother. You carried me and gave me life. I will always be grateful for that. I know I am a crime against you, an ever-present reminder of the white trash that violated you. For that I am sorry.

You must know it was not easy growing up without you, knowing that you hated me. I remember when you would come to visit Gramma Jean, I was always shuttled across the hollow to your oldest sister's house. Once when I was four, our paths crossed. Do you remember that day? You looked at me with the indifference of a stranger as I clutched Mama Sissy's hand and tried to disappear behind her. You spat on me that day when Mama Sissy told you that I was your daughter. That is my first memory of you. Sadly, the realization of who I am and what I mean to you has never changed. That was obvious today.

Did you ever look at me and just see me? When I was old enough to understand the circumstances of my conception, I cried my eyes shut. To find yourself pregnant by your rapist and have that constant reminder growing inside of you must have crippled your spirit. I heard that you wanted to abort me, but didn't. I marvel at your strength and courage to see me to term.

Or was that more Gramma Jean than you? I can't remember a family gathering where someone didn't tell the story of how you still had not looked at me two days after my birth. You just left for

Chicago, leaving Gramma Jean and Mama Sissy to raise me. Over and over I heard that your parting words to your mother and sister were "since her life matters that much to you all, you all can damn well raise her."

So many times, I wanted you to be here with me. Like when Mrs. Tillman told Gramma Jean I wasn't welcome at Sherri's birthday party because I was the half-breed bastard offspring of the town bully. Mama Sissy tried her best, but I needed your comfort. I needed you for the good times too, Mother. When I lost my first tooth, and found a Toni dollar under my pillow the next morning. I wish I could have shared that joy with you.

Did you know that most of my young life was a series of slights and rejections? Everyone knew who my father was, and I was detested because of it. Once I walked past his house and saw his mother sitting on the porch, chewing and spitting. She saw me and yelled out, "Y'all git on 'way from here, gal. Don' want your kind 'round us descent folk." I bore your shame and his offense. I faced each day with my head down, praying not to be noticed.

I often dreamed what our lives might have been if you had stayed in Stellar and raised me. Or if you had come back for me and we had lived anywhere but here. But that never happened. I hated myself for driving you away from your family. You didn't come to your own mother's funeral because I was there. I hated myself because I existed. I was proof positive of the vile and evil deed done to you.

As far back as I can remember, I would go with Mama Sissy to the wealthy homes where she'd sew dresses for the wives, mothers and daughters of the important men in Stellar. I was invisible to those people: they cared little about my parentage, they didn't view my circumstances extraordinary. They shrugged it off as being characteristic of our class. That indifferent acceptance helped keep me sane.

It wasn't until I was sixteen that someone sincerely complimented me. Not the backhanded compliments I heard about my fair skin and good hair. But an acknowledgement of something that made me worthy of existence. Mrs. Laurel Sanders – the mayor's wife – said my stitches were as fine as she'd ever seen, and I was becoming a gifted seamstress. I was overjoyed – encouraged that someone besides Gramma Jean and Mamma Sissy saw value in my existence.

That simple compliment gave me the courage, the entitlement, to pursue my passion. I worked very hard those last two years of high school, saving my money and securing a scholarship to the School of the Art Institute of Chicago. I pushed myself to excel, hoping that if – when – our paths crossed again you would be so proud of me. But that, too, never happened.

My senior year at SAIC I spent interning at a prestigious family-owned fashion house in Messina, on the island of Sicily. I was so far from Stellar and Chicago. No one knew the origins of Katherine Rodgers. No one cared. It was a blessed do over. I was innocent and untainted by my father's sins of commission and your sins of omission. Yet still, I shied away from making deep connections with my host family and coworkers. In my mind, I was not quite lovable, and they would think so too if they learned the truth.

I drifted for several years after college. I welcomed temporary assignments; it made it easier not to form attachments. I consciously chose solitude over community. I had no plans to ever fall in love. How could a decent man love and respect me? I could never marry and have children who would inherit my shame. It was enough to have a career I loved and acquaintances who bore me no ill will.

But as you know, Mother, life has a way of intervening and altering one's plans. It was my second week back in Chicago, and my first day working at the Civic Opera House as a costumer. Alessandro DiMarco, the middle son of the host family I stayed with in Sicily, was a consulting designer for Beggar's Opera. We renewed our acquaintanceship. To say that it developed into a comfortable friendship does not do justice to our relationship then or now.

To begin with, if I had ever entertained the idea of a romantic relationship with Alex, I would have rejected the idea immediately. His family is so proper. Not stuffy and condescending, just traditional, old-fashioned. For the ten months, we lived in the same house, not once did Alex insinuate himself in my life — there was not even the slightest flirtation. And he is so incredibly handsome, Mother. Six-year old girls and widows of sixty shamelessly flirt with him. I also was infatuated with him. As we grew closer over months of collaboration, those schoolgirl feelings matured. They were a secret fantasy I would never acknowledge.

One evening, several weeks before the opening of Beggar's Opera, Alex and I were reviewing requests for costume changes. Without preamble, Alex turned to me and said, "I wish to escort you to the party after the opening performance. Will you permit me your company?"

I answered, "Of course. That is until you find someone you'd rather go with to the party."

Alex cut me off with a sharp "No!" He had never raised his voice at me before; he had never been so abrupt. I was shocked. Then he gently told me, "Kitty, I did not ask you to be a placeholder. It is your company I desire. No one else's. Do you not feel just a little of the pleasure you bring to me?"

Tears flowed unrestrained as I poured out my heart to Alex that night. I told him about my inauspicious beginnings. I confessed why I would never allow the love I felt for him to grow beyond the friendship we shared. All the while I expected Alex to recoil and retract his invitation. Instead he wiped my tears and took my hand in his.

"Let me share with you a family secret my dear Kitty," he said. "My oldest sister Nicolette was present at our parents' wedding."

My brain was so muddled from the confession and sobbing that I didn't understand what Alex was saying.

"My dearest," he began again, "Papa already had put the bun in Mama's oven when they took their vows. Neither is ashamed, nor do they claim Nicolette as premature. It is life; it is accepted."

And then he spoke the words that lifted the agonizing weight from my heart. "What that red-necked coward did to your mother was barbaric, what happened to your mother is indeed tragic, but what they allowed to be your life is unconscionable. As your friend and champion, I will never allow anyone to disparage you.

"I love and adore you Katherine Jean Rodgers. Your smile, your essence, it comes from your innocent heart. It is so genuine that my world lights up in its presence. It draws me to you and overshadows even the perfection of your physical beauty."

You see, Mother, I had never really seen me. I had only seen me through the eyes of others too eager to attribute to me the sins of my parents. When I saw me through Alex's eyes, I was amazed. And I liked what I saw.

And then, Mother, he promised, "When one day you honor me and become Kitty DiMarco, I will remind you every day of my life that you are a treasure."

Alex held me in his arms and kissed me — a kiss so filled with love and passion that my knees buckled. It was our first kiss, my first real kiss ever, and all I could think was encore, encore.

Mother, I write this letter to tell you that I have missed you all my life, to tell you some of the things I have wanted to share with you. I write to tell you I no longer crave the life I did not have with you. I no longer need your forgiveness or acceptance. I have learned to love Kitty DiMarco just the way she is.

Mother, allow me to introduce you to your daughter. She is an accomplished artist, designer and costumer. She is a beloved wife and expectant mother. She is embraced by her husband's family. She has friendships, and is a cherished friend. She is strong and brave. She is happy. I have learned to like her and to love her. It is regrettable that you never knew her. You would have liked and loved her, too.

I thank you for giving me life.

May you find peace now,

Katherine Jean Rodgers DiMarco

Alex refolded the pages and slipped them back into the envelope. His eyes were moist and his throat husky as he said, "you remember well our first night. I had never wanted anything more in my life. Your love, your trust in me, complete me. I will never want anything more."

Kitty kissed him. As he had kissed her that first time. This was her life.

When their lips parted, Alex asked, "what now, Kitty?"

Kitty smiled. "I bury this with her," she said of the letter. She placed Alex's hand on the small mound that was overtaking her waistline. "Then we go home, il mio amore. We go home."

Kick me when I'm down
Only pushes me to prove
It ain't over yet

Best Seller

Every writer dreams of penning a best seller. Don't ever be fooled by modest assertions of "I just write for the fun of it." People who write just for the fun of it keep diaries that are never mentioned in life. The grandchildren discover those diaries in an attic one summer a decade after their death and the children blog said diaries as a tribute, though it's more often done to soothe their guilt for neglecting the parent during his/her twilight years.

Being a published writer, i.e., an author, justifies all the copious amounts of coffee consumed and time squandered while staring at a blank page or the blinking insertion point on its digital counterpart. One dreams of emerging from self-imposed exile in the Room of Ten Thousand Sticky Notes with THE manuscript that sends staid publishers into a bidding war frenzy.

I was no different. That was my life and my dream.

My name is Josie Sinclair. Yes, that Josie Sinclair, indie author and publisher of the best seller, *The Absolute Nothingness of a Too Full Plate.* My "groundbreaking" critically acclaimed novel has been blowing up the traditional and digital circuits for the last eighteen months. Yes, eighteen months! Can you believe it? Bookstores can't keep the title on their shelves. It's downloaded continuously throughout the day. So far, it's been translated into Spanish and Italian. And now Hollywood is knocking on the door, tempting me with checks bearing a stupefying number of zeros, and begging yours truly to write the screen adaptation.

If you're wondering if the rumor is true – it is. I wrote *The Absolute Nothingness of a Too Full Plate* over a weekend. It's even more amazing than it sounds. Let me take you back to where it all began.

When I was growing up, I had three living generations of role models to emulate. The problem, and it would continue to be a problem as an undergrad, was that I couldn't decide on a single career. To complicate matters, the more I was exposed to different career choices, the more noncommittal I became. Six years after entering the University of Chicago, I had completed major requirements for three degrees – cum laude, by the way – and still had no inkling as to what I wanted to pursue as a career. I was fascinated by everything, and attacked its mastery with fervor, only to push it to the back burner and move on to the next captivating vocation that hijacked my attention.

"Enough is enough!" I remember my Mom telling me. "Graduate, pick a grad school and chart a career already. Hell, get a job – I don't give a flying saucer!"

Mom's words instantly triggered the muse in me. Images of a young woman getting a broken-down space shuttle for her eighteenth birthday, painstakingly restoring it, and eventually saving the world from alien domination and destruction flitted across my mind.

That was my 'aha' moment. I had grown up and finally knew what I wanted to be. I would be a writer. I could be everything I wanted to be in the fictional worlds I created. This career choice was pure genius.

I took the next necessary step to authorship and applied to the prestigious MFA creative writing program at Hunter College in New York. Two years later, having honed my craft, armed with a degree, industry contacts and ideas galore, I returned to Chicago to take up residence in a Rogers Park studio.

Over the next three years I produced novels and short stories at an impressive rate, while holding down various jobs to pay the rent: substitute teacher, receptionist, barista, sales clerk. I was living the life of a starving artist. What was truly impressive, and my claim to fame during that period, is that one of my submissions received a whopping thirty-one rejections. I refused to take rejection personally, though. Even after *Harry Potter* made her very bankable, J. K. Rowling still got rejection letters. I just hunkered down, plied my craft and hung on to the dream.

One weekend twenty months ago, I was in an uncharacteristically melancholy mood. Sales – and as a result, hours and commissions – were down at the boutique I clerked at, and I had received a rejection letter that was gnawing at my spirit. In a terse twenty-two words, I was told to pick my publishers more carefully in the future, and write in the genre I claimed. By the time I had finished two bottles of Pinot Grigio, I was mad as hell and in full throttle "I'll show you" mode.

I extracted every hard copy of my manuscripts from the piles of papers stacked around the apartment. I unclipped, unstapled, unbound and otherwise separated the pages. I tossed them in the air.

The result was mounds of single sheets scattered over the floor. I knelt and shuffled them around a bit, randomly selecting 500 pages, numbering them with a Sharpie as I went along.

I brought the ream to my computer, opened a new Word document, and the document my hard copy page one came from. I found that page in the document and copied it into my new Word document. I continued "writing" my manuscript in this manner. When finished, I drifted from the wine induced mania into a deep snoring slumber.

~=~=~=~=~=~=~

A massive headache and an overachieving sun ushered in the next day. I found myself in a field of paper, clutching a page with 500 written in the upper left margin.

"What the hell happened?" The sound of my voice – even at that normal conversational decibel – was painful enough to push me further down into the field of paper.

From this ground zero vantage point, I surveyed the two-hundredths of an acre I called home. It looked like some sick printer had upchucked all over the apartment.

I sat up. Too quick. As I brought my hand up to still the reverberations in my head, memories of the night before confronted me. The pity, the wine, the writing.

My creative soul was curious to see the result of that volatile cocktail, while common sense urged me to clean up the reams of paper I had fool heartedly rained down on my innocent abode.

Prioritize I told my hungover self. Silently this time.

The first order of business became neutralizing the battering ram running amok in my head. I stumbled over to the kitchen area and washed down two bananas with a half-liter of Sprite. I put on the kettle and readied my mug for a ginger tea chaser. Next, I filled four 13-gallon trash bags with paper. Finally, with my teabag steeping, I turned to my faithful computer.

I read the familiar words on the screen, out of context – but strangely profound. Five pages into this mashup, I knew I had hit upon something big, which is what I initially called the manuscript. I began reformatting the text, cleaning up the page breaks and selecting a font. I tweaked the names and locations, making them consistent throughout. I smoothed out the page transitions to obliterate the disjointed feel.

I edited, saved and printed *Something Big* several times before taking a power nap in the afternoon.

Over the next twenty-eight hours I worked nonstop on *Something Big*, stopping only to refuel with coffee. When Monday morning dawned, I had 465 double-spaced, one-inch margined pages which now had a cover page and the title: *The Absolute Nothingness of a Too Full Plate.*

I established myself as an indie publisher, marketed my book my way, and the rest, as they say in the business, is history.

Ask me what I think
I'm bound to tell you the truth
I love you that much

Fed Up

"You're fat. Not pleasingly plump, or plus-sized or any other polite euphemism. You're overweight and it is not pregnancy weight. Your obesity threatens to leave me a widower and our son without a mother."

Althea Bryant, my wife's relationship counselor, stares at me in disbelief.

Jasmine's mouth drops open. "How could you be so mean?"

"You insisted that I attend this session with this overpriced therapist. You wanted my honest opinion about you weight and our marriage. Well now you've got them!"

"Sam, perhaps we should choose words that aren't so inflammatory," Althea says, leaning forward to flash me a peek at her double-D cleavage.

"Don't start with me, lady. You sit there with your playmate body, dressed like a vamp. What's with that? Are you trying to make my wife feel unattractive? You know she's going to make the comparison. My guess is that you get off flaunting your stuff at these sessions. It's your sick little power trip."

"I sense your anger is an attempt to mask your inadequacy..."

"Shut your mouth. Right now." My words and look warn Althea that I mean business.

I look over at Jasmine. The range of emotions cycling across her face remind me why I agreed to this absurd counseling session with this non-credentialed wannabe. I wanted neutral ground – someplace Jasmine and I would never find ourselves at again – to deliver the hard punches necessary to get us back on track.

"You only have pity sex with me," Jasmine weeps.

"That's not true."

"When was the last time you wanted to have sex with me?" she challenges.

I look at my watch. "Fourteen minutes ago – when we were walking into the building. If you'd turned around you'd have seen a boner that rivaled the Grand Teton peak. I love your ass – even carrying the extra weight.

"Before that it was this morning when I overheard you ordering flowers to send to my parents on my birthday next week. I love your generosity. The way you make my parents feel like they haven't lost a son, but gained a daughter.

"And before that..."

"You never say anything."

"When I do, you're either tired or distracted. When we do have sex, you look like you're in pain, or you just want to hurry up and get it over with. I can't get off at the expense of your discomfort – physical or emotional. I'd rather spend time with my hand."

"I thought you found someone else. That I don't appeal to you anymore."

"I'm a simple man, Jazz. I can't compartmentalize like that. Love and sex are all in the same Jasmine bucket. If I think about either of them, I think about you. I don't want it any other way. I love you. I'm in love with you."

"Then why are you so distant?"

"Because it hurts when I think about us ending. About you eating yourself into bad health and an early grave."

"I only eat because I feel so...I don't know...fat and ugly."

"This is good. You two are communicating..."

"Shut up," we both tell Althea.

We end the session early. On the way out, I tell Althea's stud muffin receptionist not to book any more sessions. "We're done."

~=~=~=~=~=~=~=~

"How can we be done?" Jazz asks as we navigate midday Saturday traffic. "I'm still forty pounds overweight and you're still distant."

We drive in silence the rest of the way home. We sit in the car in the driveway, neither of us ready to take a step back into our world.

"Okay. These are the ground rules," I announce. "Rule one, whenever I want to have sex with you, I'll tell you. Or show you. It's up to you whether we do or not." I try to look really hurt, but not manipulative, at the possibility of rejection.

"Rule two, whenever you feel like eating to compensate for anything other than hunger, have sex with me. I guarantee I won't turn you down, and I'll make you feel like the sexiest woman on earth." Jazz's eyes sparkle. I love her eyes.

"Rule three, starting tonight we keep working on finding just the right sweet spot to insure maximum mutual satisfaction. We may have to put in a lot of time and energy to find it, or them – it's always best to have a fallback position or two – but it'll be worth it. I'm all in. What about you, Jazz?"

"And what if we're nowhere near each other when the urge for sex or food hits?"

"We hold the thought. I do know where you live."

"You're so silly, Sam. It sounds like all you have on your mind is sex."

Jazz hasn't called me silly in such a long time. I miss that.

"Yeah. I'm a man. Your man. I love you. I want to make love with you. Only you. I want to have sex with you until both of us are too old and senile to remember what sex is, or I'm a hundred and twenty – whichever comes first. Did I mention sex is good for burning calories and keeping the heart fit? You do want to keep my heart fit? Don't you?"

Jazz smiles. I love that smile. It's a smile I haven't seen much of lately. It's a smile I'm going to do everything in my power to see a whole lot more of it in the future.

I can't remember
Love between us without pain
Maybe now, at last

Remembering Michael

Estranged? Lena knew what the word meant, and she realized what it implied. She had not faced it before this moment – had not admitted that she and Michael were estranged. She thought back to the times when they were together. Pain, his or hers, whether physical or emotional, defined those times. Lena had rationalized their lack of everyday involvement in one another's life as a natural drifting apart. What was the adage? A son is a son until he takes a wife. And there had always been a 'wife' of some sorts. Since he was thirteen there had been a succession of girlfriends, wives, live-in lovers – their initial presence exalted, their departure vilified.

"Were you and your son estranged? How did you come to have a gun with you? Had you been quarreling?" This new set of questions brought Lena back to the present.

"I suppose we are estranged." Lena looked around the apartment. Police officers and medical personnel busied themselves assessing and recording the sorrowful scene. "Were," she corrected herself.

Michael's body already had been lifted onto a gurney, carried down the stairs and loaded into the waiting ambulance, which had slowly, silently pulled away from the curb. No need to rush – Michael was beyond any help this world could offer.

"Mrs. Taylor, help me to understand why you shot your son," Detective Dan Robbins said, his voice hushed, his tone soothing.

Lena didn't answer. She saw in her mind's eye the paramedics meticulously working on Michael's lifeless body. Lena wondered if they could have succeeded in giving Michael life again if she had not failed him repeatedly, had not always disappointed him.

"Why don't we sit over here?" Detective Robbins suggested, leading Lena Taylor over to the sofa. "Those will have to stay on," he nodded at the handcuffs binding Lena's wrists together. He sat down beside her.

Lena could see most of the apartment from where she sat on the sofa. Directly in front of her, adjacent to the front door, was the kitchen. Take out containers overflowed from the trash bin onto the floor. To her left was the small bedroom, mattress on the floor, no box springs or bed frame. An upside-down Rubbermaid bin provided a makeshift nightstand. Next to it was an overturned jug of sweet tea and a half empty bottle of antifreeze. The remnants of the deadly cocktail sat in a glass on top of the bin. An empty prescription bottle of Tylenol with codeine – hers from when she had broken her ankle last winter – lay on its side next to the glass. Lena had stopped taking the pills once the pain was bearable. Now she wished she'd gotten rid of the pills properly.

"Mrs. Taylor, I know this is difficult, but I need to understand why you shot your son," Detective Robbins broached the subject again.

Lena shook her head. "You know when Michael was born the doctors weren't sure if he'd live past six. He had a hole in his heart that was inoperable. It left Michael delicate. He couldn't run and play like the other kids. He was ten years old the first time he told me he hated me. Michael said it was my defective womb that crippled his heart. You know his father accused me of the exact same thing when he left me."

What a prick, Robbins thought, *like father like son*. "Yes, Ma'am. About the shooting."

Lena ignored Robbins' probe. "Michael was always battling something. If it wasn't him battling life, he was battling himself or someone else. Most of the time that someone was me. You know, when he went away to college he pretended I was dead. Pretended he was an orphan with a trust fund. Truth be told, Michael had a full scholarship – something he should've been proud of, but it wasn't enough. Michael worked all through high school – after school, summers and weekends – to get the money for all the extras to support that invented lifestyle. Pledged himself to a snobby fraternity. I didn't find out until I paid him a surprise visit. How was I to know? If I had known, I would have stayed away. I never wanted to hurt Michael."

Lena paused and shuddered. "When I came to the house, his fraternity brothers told me I had the wrong Michael Taylor. It wasn't until I insisted and showed them pictures of me and Michael that they told me Michael's lies. The confrontation was ugly. Michael said I was a mental case, a crazy friend of his dead mother, that my grief over the loss of my son caused me to substitute Michael for him."

Lena sighed heavily before continuing. "He was kicked out of the fraternity. Pretty much everyone on campus shunned him. He dropped out and took up with Carmen and her family. One look and you knew they were poor trash. Bunch of con artists to boot. But Michael embraced them, they played to his vanity. He ended up marrying the girl. Turned out she was underage and that was the only way her daddy wasn't filing statutory rape charges. He did a lot of bad things with that lot. If only I could've afforded a better lawyer or made restitution. But I couldn't. Michael went to prison for a time."

"Perhaps we can start with how you got the gun." Robbins had interviewed many Lena Taylors over the years. Each had an insatiable need to unload the years of crap that brought them to this place. Usually, he'd just bide his time – the confession always came sooner or later. Tonight, he really wanted it to be sooner so he could go home and wash off the day's stench.

"Never felt the need to have a gun in the city before. Back home in Russellville I had a riffle. I would go hunting with my Pa and brothers. I was a pretty good shot then. That was a long time ago. My aim is off now."

"The gun you used this evening, where did it come from, Mrs. Taylor?"

"Did you know Michael tried to kill himself twice before?"

"No Ma'am." *Maybe if I let her tell the story at her pace I'll get answers to my questions,* Robbins reasoned. "Can you tell me about the first time your son attempted suicide?"

"It was after an argument he had with his wife Lorraine. Lorraine was wife number three. A really pretty girl – outgoing, confident, never 'fraid to speak her mind, but always in a nice respectful way. Well, she and Michael got into a fight. Never knew about what. She left. When she returned she found him in a pool of blood – his wrists cut. Poor Lorraine. She felt so guilty, felt responsible. She had wanted to leave, but she stayed. Michael never let her forget – browbeat that girl till she was a mousy shadow of herself. Then he left her."

The distaste was clearly evident in his expression. Robbins usually felt sympathy for suicide victims. The despair and hopelessness felt at that moment when death was judged preferable to life must be overwhelming. But Robbins didn't like Michael Taylor; he felt no sympathy for Michael Taylor. In his mind's eye, Michael Taylor was a lying, manipulating piece of shit.

The uniformed officer – young and female – stationed within earshot of Robbins and Mrs. Taylor, shifted the weight of her gun belt as she approached the pair. She had just finished talking on her cellphone, and now she leaned over and whispered in Robbins' ear, glancing occasionally at Lena Taylor.

"And Dr. Stevens is sure?" responded Robbins.

"Yes sir," the officer replied.

Robbins turned his attention back to Lena Taylor. "Tell me more about Michael," he said to her. He had resolved not to rush whatever she wanted to say.

"I should have come yesterday. He called me." Lena sighed. It was hard for Lena to admit that Michael only called to blame her for whatever drama he found himself in. "I could hear the sadness in his voice. It was familiar."

"What did he say?" Robbins asked.

Lena brought her cuffed hands up to her face and began massaging her eyes.

"I think we can do without those," he said to the young officer, motioning to the handcuffs.

The officer removed the handcuffs and went back to her post.

Lena folded her hands meekly in her lap. "Michael called early yesterday, around four in the morning. He was all upset about this new girl he was dating. Seems she knew someone who was a cousin to one of his exes. She called him out about his ways. He tried to explain it away with the ex being vindictive because he broke it off. That's when the girl told him she had run a background check on him. She used her business to verify his financials, and did some public record sleuthing. She found out about his prison time and some of the other lies – the main one being that his cash was always short because he was keeping me in a fancy home where I could have quality round-the-clock nursing care. She found out that I live in my own home, mortgage free."

Robbins added *deadbeat* to the list of Michael's attributes. "You loved your son – didn't you Mrs. Taylor?"

"Oh, yes! I love Michael dearly. I carried him under my heart for nine months; he's been on my heart ever since. He's not all bad. He just has a hard time reconciling who he is with who he wants to be. I know he bends the truth to favor him, but he believes that if you speak it out into the universe, it will manifest itself. He just wants to be...someone else."

Robbins drew in a deep breath and exhaled slowly. *Every opportunity that asshole had he was manifesting death and infirmity for his mother. Didn't she see how hateful he was?*

Robbins and Lena Taylor sat silently for a while. He finally broke the silence. "Why did you come here this evening?"

"I tried calling Michael all day but never got an answer. I just felt in my heart that he was in trouble. I should have come yesterday. I just kept going through yesterday and today like everything was normal. I knew something was wrong. I could feel it. I let him down again. I ignored his cry for help."

"Mrs. Taylor, there was no way you could have known his intentions."

"A mother knows. In the back of my mind I knew."

They sat in silence again.

Lena continued. "When I got here, I used my key. The chain was on the door. I pushed hard and managed to tear it away from the frame. They were on him when I came in. Eight, ten of them. They were gnawing on his nose and eyes and fingers. I took the gun from my purse and started shooting." Lena's eyes were brimming with tears. She looked up at the ceiling, perhaps the heavens. "I couldn't even do that right. I didn't mean to shoot Michael. I was trying to kill the rats."

This confirmed what his initial assessment of the crime scene revealed and what the young officer had told Robbins: Michael Taylor had sustained post mortem rodent bites on his face and extremities, and the bullets that pierced his heart and skull were not the cause of death. His organs had already shut down from the antifreeze and drugs.

Robbins placed a comforting hand over Lena's. "Mrs. Taylor, this has been quite an ordeal. I'll have Officer Lewis drive you home." He beckoned for the young officer. Robbins truly felt badly for Lena Taylor, but he was not going to tell her he was sorry for her loss. He wasn't sorry. *Good riddance to bad rubbish.*

Officer Lewis helped Lena Taylor to her feet, out the apartment and down to the patrol car. Seated in the back of the car, Lena thought about the unanswered questions about the gun.

Should she tell the truth, the whole truth and nothing but the truth, she would have to say she bought the gun for Michael because she was wearied of his failed attempts. She would have to say that she had had enough – that if Michael really wanted to kill himself she would give him the gun to do it. And she would have to say she regretted that thought the moment she saw her baby's body being eaten away by those rats. That was the whole truth. *So help me God.*

But for now, Lena Taylor would say nothing more and just remember Michael as he could have been.

It's simple, Simon
Remember what I tell you
Well, most of the time

Simon Forgets

"I want to have an affair," Simon says.

My handsome husband of forty-seven days says this as casually as if it were "please past the salt."

My heart catches in my throat. *Had I done something wrong?* Simon and I had eloped after knowing each other only two weeks. It was the most impulsive thing I had ever done. But it just seemed so right. It is right.

We had met on one of those 6-day, 5-night cruises promoting timeshares. Simon seduced me with his guilelessness, while impressing me with his investment acumen. In three days, he turned a $7000 profit on my $500 investment. The man sure knew how to make money!

We were so happy on that cruise. We're happy now. *Aren't we? Had it been too soon? Was the honeymoon — and the marriage — over?*

Now I muster the courage to meet his dreamy brown eyes and ask, "hypothetically, or do you have someone in mind?" *Please don't let it be my sister*, I silently pray.

"Definitely not hypothetical," he replies, happily. "I want to have an affair with you. It's on my to do list."

You can hear the relief in my sigh. I do a double take of this gorgeous man and say, "hello, I'm Christina. Your wife. Remember?"

I say this only half in jest. Simon has proven to be a savant when it comes to investing, and the absentminded professor in all other areas of his life. He routinely forgets where he puts things, even forgetting to look at the notes I've pinned inside his pockets reminding him of things he needs to remember. His brain routinely takes detours where no other brain has gone before.

"I know who you are, Chrissy," Simon says with good natured indignation. "I was just thinking how much fun it would be to have clandestine meetings in downtown hotels and out of the way places."

Umm — a little role playing couldn't hurt. It could be fun. "Any place in mind for this fantasy adventure?"

"Maybe. I saw this Groupon…"

Simon is so charming as he says this, but I know where this is heading, and I don't have the time to plan this fantasy. Sisters Boutique has inventory and a buying trip before the pre-Black Friday sales in three weeks. My plate is overflowing. And when Simon immerses himself in anything, it is seldom straightforward. I can only imagine how long and convoluted the process had been before he realized he wanted some romantic alone time with me before the rush of the holidays. After all, his lead-in was "I want to have an affair."

"I'll let you take care of the details, Simon. Just tell me where, when and what to pack."

He smiles and pulls me into his arms. "I love you so much, Chrissy. I'll do anything to keep you happy and in love with me." His kiss underscores his words. "I'll call later with a plan."

~=~=~=~=~=~=~=~

Later comes without the phone call. Simon shows up at the end of the day in a junk heap of a car.

My sister, Millicent, and I come out of the boutique to inspect the eyesore at the curb.

Excitedly Simon tells us, "I got it at one of those pay where you buy lots. It was only $450."

"That may not have been a bargain," Millicent says, as she examines the rust on the rust.

"I'm not sure how this figures into a romantic getaway," I say.

"Oh, I forgot to call, didn't I," Simon says, talking more to himself than to me. He switches gears quickly. "Picture this: newlyweds on their way to a weekend hideaway in their sleek new sports car."

"Hate to burst your bubble," Millicent interrupts, "but that is not a sleek new sports car."

Simon gives her an exasperated look. "I know that. Anyway, they stop for supper at a roadside diner and their car is stolen. Undaunted, they buy an old beat up car from the only gas station for miles to continue their journey. On the way, they're forced to…"

Now I interrupt. "Okay. I'll give you high marks for creative backstory, but really, Simon, do you think this car has even another ten miles in its future?"

"Oh, sure Chrissy. The salesman guaranteed the engine is in tiptop shape."

Millicent and I exchange a bemused look. "Where does he come up with these ideas, Chrissy?" she mocks.

I give Millicent the stink eye. Nicknames are never used in our family. Mother disapproves of them.

"Be nice," I tell her.

"I found this B & B near Kettle Moraine. They don't have Groupons though," he adds, as if that might be a deal breaker.

"I'm sure it'll be just fine. When are we leaving, and what should I pack?"

"Now," Simon says enthusiastically. "Hiking boots, a pair of jeans, that invisible tank top and lacy boy shorts I like, that oversized sweater that feels so good to cuddle up to, silk scarves, chocolate sauce…"

I feel my face flush. "Okay, Simon." I cut him off before he continues with the fantasy wardrobe.

Millicent says nothing, but the urge to wisecrack is written all over her face.

"I've already packed everything you need." He gestures at my DK weekender sitting on the back seat of the car next to his canvass-strapped leather duffle. "I promise it will be fun. Please," he begs like an impatient toddler, "can we go? Now?"

Simon's invitation is irresistible. His unabashed eagerness is contagious. "Give me ten minutes," I tell him, while dragging Millicent back into the shop.

Millicent is grinning from ear to ear and shaking her head.

"What!"

"Oh, nothing. It's just two months ago, you wouldn't have even considered doing something this spontaneous. Simon's good for you."

"I take that to mean you don't mind holding down the fort this weekend while I…"

"Have incredibly hot sex with that hunky husband of yours in some romantic hideaway. Yes, I mind cause I'm rocking this whole sibling rivalry thing. I'm major league jealous of you two.

"Bottom line, though, is I'm happy you're happy. It's about time you cut loose and walk on the wild side, Christina. You don't always have to be the super responsible one. I can handle things here. And Rita is coming in tomorrow, so I'll have help.

"I only have one request – find out if he has a brother, or a cousin. Heck, if he's anything like Simon, I might consider trading in Micah." Micah is my sister's longtime benefits buddy.

Millicent's request reminds me of how little I know about my husband. Does Simon have siblings? Our relationship is missing some basic background information.

"Did I say something wrong, Christina?" Millicent asks, genuinely concerned by my furrowed brow.

I hug my sister. "No. Just a newlywed reality check, I guess. Lots of uncharted territory here."

"Then don't keep the man waiting. Go chart!" Millicent pushes me out the door.

Simon sprints to the passenger car door and creaks it open and shut for me.

As we pull into traffic, I turn to see my sister smiling and waving me off to a romantic weekend adventure. I can get used to this life. I settle back to enjoy the ride.

~=~=~=~=~=~=~=~

Halfway into the two-and-a-half-hour drive, we stop at a diner to stretch and use the facilities. Simon insists we sit side-by-side in a booth and share a slice of apple pie à la mode with caramel sauce. I learn that it is Simon's second favorite desert. He says I am his favorite.

There's a couple with three young girls in the diner. The girls are dressed in their favorite princess costumes, and the parents are toting a backpack from which extra clothes, favorite toys, sippy cups, animal crackers and wet washcloths emerge.

Simon is mesmerized by their chaos. He pulls me closer. "We must have babies. Lots of them."

My heart does backflips. At thirty-five, I have had my share of relationships – good, bad and forgettable ones. And ones I wish I could forget. Never has there been a man like Simon in my life, and I doubt there has ever been a relationship quite like ours.

When we leave the diner, much to my disappointment, no one has stolen the car.

~=~=~=~=~=~=~=~=~

On the road again, nearly five hours after leaving Chicago, we are still nowhere near our destination. Or maybe we are. Who can tell? Our vehicle is sans a navigation system, and both of our smartphones need a charge – no USB charging ports in this ancient vehicle. The backup directions that Simon googled and printed are – wait for it – forgotten at home in the printer's output tray.

It's getting dark, and it feels like we are wandering the same winding backroad for the nth time.

"I think I've gotten us lost, Chrissy. We should stop and ask for directions," Simon suggests.

"That's a good idea," I agree. *How can I be annoyed with Simon, who readily admits his folly and is ready to set things right?*

We look around. It would be an even better idea if there was someone to ask.

Stranded on a single-track dirt road, just as night settles in, surrounded by the remnants of harvested corn fields, is anything but romantic. It's downright eerie. If it weren't for the supermoon hovering overhead, I'm certain we wouldn't be able to see our own outstretched hands. Or those of the zombies lying in wait.

"This land has to belong to someone," Simon reasons. "This field didn't harvest itself. I bet we can get help from whoever farms this land."

Simon puts the car in park and gets out. I follow. He jumps on the hood and climbs up on the roof. The car creaks and moans under his weight as he surveys our location from this new vantage point.

"Over there," he points. "There's a house over there."

I resist the urge to comment that I can see the exact same thing from where I'm standing on the ground.

"How do we get there?" I ask. "We can't just go driving through someone's corn field. Can we?"

"I don't see why not. It's not like we'd be mowing down their crops. The combines have already been through here. Whatever is left is waste."

Simon jumps down from the roof to the hood, leaving a sizable dent before sliding to the ground.

We get back in the car. Barely a hundred yards into our rerouted journey, I'm startled by a large boom followed by hissing. The car swerves, and there is a boom-boom and more hissing. The car does not move forward now. Simon again puts the car in park and gets out. He walks around the car. On his second orbit, he opens my door and takes my hand to coax me out.

"We've got three flats, Chrissy," Simon says.

"What do we do now?" I'm on the brink of panic and try not to whine.

"We're gonna have to walk the rest of the way." Simon thinks for a minute. "We leave the headlights and high beams on to help guide us. Then we walk."

"Won't that drain the battery?"

"Probably. It doesn't matter since we're not going anywhere tonight on these flats. We can get a tow and a jump in the morning. I think our plan for tonight is getting to that house over there."

Simon reaches in and gets my bag off the backseat. "You don't want to walk in those," he says pointing to my sculpted heels. "Put on your boots. They'll be easier to walk in. You see what the dead stalks did to the tires. Besides there might be rats running around."

"You're kidding, right?"

"Nope. Course odds are the field is baited with poison, so it might be just dead rats. Course there are always survivors. Rats adapt well. And then sometimes farmers use owls or falcons to control rodent populations. Who knows? Better to be safe."

My head is swimming. I desperately want to be somewhere else. Preferably inside with a cozy fire, a four-poster bed and lots of down comforters.

I sit back down in the car, door open, to change from shoes to boots. Before I can bend to lace and tie my boots, Simon is on his knees, performing the task for me. *How can I stay annoyed with a man who is just so sweet and even-tempered?*

When he finishes, Simon grabs both bags and my hand, and we set out across the field by the light of the car headlights and the supermoon.

Thankfully, the trek across the field is uneventful: no rodent attacks, animal carcasses or swooping predators. We emerge from the field yards from the house. I can see light shining through the curtained windows as we approach. Aside from the house, there are outlines of other buildings – livestock and grain barns, I suppose.

Simon walks up the stairs and knocks on the door of the house. I am close behind.

After the longest minute, the door opens. A weather worn screen door still separates us from the couple on the other side. His face is without expression; hers is grim. Perhaps it is the wheelchair she sits in that dictates her demeanor.

"We're lost," I blurt out.

"Come in," the woman says. She wheels backwards, and the man holds open the screen door. "Come in," she repeats. "You surprised us. We didn't hear a car."

"We came across the field," Simon points. The couple peers around us at the dimming lights of the car. "I'm Simon, and this is my wife Chrissy."

"Indeed," the woman looks at me. The introduction seems to bother her. Her lips smile, though. "I'm Antonia. This is Jake."

Simon drops our bags by the door. They usher us into an old-fashioned parlor. "Bring the tea, Pet," Antonia instructs Jake, just as he is about to sit down. "Please, sit down," she says to Simon and me.

Jake rushes off to get the tea, while Simon and I sit together on the settee across from Antonia.

She watches the way Simon holds my hand. She says nothing. I am uncomfortable with the silence.

Simon moves closer to me and says, "Chrissy and I are heading up to The Cottages near Kettle Moraine."

"We got married six weeks ago," I add. "Every weekend is a honeymoon adventure."

"How nice for you," Antonia says.

I'm babbling. I sound like an idiot. *Could I possibly make a worse impression?*

"I must have taken a wrong turn," Simon continues. "I saw this house from the backroad. We were headed across the field to ask directions, when we got a flat."

"Actually, we got three flats. Can you believe it?" *I need to shut up before I say something unredeemable. Why am I so flustered?*

Jake returns carrying a tray, which he sets on the coffee table. He pours fragrant tea from a traditional china pot into delicate cups with matching saucers. He sits on the footstool beside Antonia, looking at her adoringly.

I add four sugar cubes to the cup Antonia has handed me, stir, sip, then deciding I like the taste, finish off the tea in a few swallows. Everyone is watching me.

"This is really good tea." I hope the compliment redeems my gluttonous behavior. I feel like I'm flattering a supplier who's decided that I'm not big enough to do business with.

"I see," Antonia says.

"It's really delicious," I reiterate.

Jake gets up and refills my cup. Everyone watches as I dissolve four more cubes in my tea.

I begin to feel more relaxed. The tea is warm and comforting. I watch Jake and Antonia. *What an odd couple.* Antonia appears to be around my age, give or take a couple of years. She is petite. Her hair is bone straight – an unnatural shade of black that could only come from a bottle. Her hair is pulled into a tight ponytail. Antonia is pale – not fair or sickly pale, but the kind of pallor that comes from years of sunless days. Her lipstick is much too red, and seems out of context in these surroundings.

Jake is tall – Simon's height. He seems shy and easygoing. His light brown hair is sun-kissed and graying at the temples. The rolled-up sleeves of his shirt reveal the toned muscles acquired by hard physical labor. He seems to worship Antonia. I giggle. *She calls him Pet.*

My giggling interrupts the silence. I switch my empty cup for Simon's nearly full one. Simon smiles as I finish his tea to which I've added three cubes of sugar.

Antonia watches intently, no doubt sizing me – us – up as I have just done with her and Jake.

I yawn and glance at the clock on the mantle. Antonia follows my gaze.

"You must be tired. It's much too late to have anyone service your car. You will stay the night."

Both Jake and Simon seem relieved by Antonia's decision.

"Show them the guest room, Pet."

Simon and I stand; I am a bit unsteady. Simon swoops me up in his arms, as Antonia wheels herself to the staircase. Jake carries Antonia up the stairs. Simon follows him, carrying me. At the top, Jake points to a room at the opposite end of the hall and we part company. I am asleep as soon as my head hits the pillow.

~=~=~=~=~=~=~=~

I'm having the most delicious dream. Simon is kissing my neck. His kisses are hot and passionate. His kisses trail down to meet his hand which is cupping my breast. His fingers caress my nipple and then his mouth devours it. His tongue teases it. The feeling is wonderful. I don't want to wake up.

"You taste so good," Simon says as he suckles, caresses.

"Stop talking." The female voice is cold, harsh. *Did I say that?*

I'm somewhere between dreamland and real land. I try to adjust to my surroundings. My arms and legs feel strange. I look and see they are tied to the bedposts. *What creative playtime has Simon imagined? I must remember to tell Millicent that the Italian silk scarves are a very wise purchase.*

"Get down!"

"Yes, Mistress Toni," I hear Simon say as he backs off the bed and kneels obediently beside Antonia. He's wearing a dog collar and his magnificent manhood is caged. *This is by far the darkest dream I've ever had!*

Antonia sits there in her wheelchair, the quintessential dominatrix in leather lingerie, wielding a whip. She turns to Jake and commands, "pierce her now!"

I try to raise my head to see what is happening. Jake approaches the bed. He's naked, too. Except for his dog collar and cock cage. *This is one kinky dream.*

Jake clamps my erect left nipple between something metal, a needle is pushed through my nipple, and…

"Omigod!" My voice squeaks.

This is not a dream. I feel everything: the pinching of the cold metal clamp, the pain of the needle tearing through my nipple, the pressure of a rod pushing through, the sensation of turning – like thumbscrews.

I struggle to get up; I am bound too tightly to the bed to move more than a couple of inches. My head aches – as if it is channeling every hangover since the beginning of time. I can't find my voice to scream, to protest. Tears pool and run out of the corners of my eyes.

"Simon."

He doesn't look at me. His head remains bowed. I feel the prick in my arm, and then nothing.

~=~=~=~=~=~=~=~

My mouth is so dry. I feel like part of me is swimming. I'm sitting with my back to the headboard – still bound spread eagle to the bed. The silk scarves at my wrists and ankles have been replaced with shackles.

Jake is sponging my piercing. It is at once erotic and invasive. I try yanking my hands from the cuffs. They don't budge. I want to cover myself. I am wearing only the sheer lace boy shorts that Simon loves. I might as well be naked as they conceal nothing.

"Where's Simon? Why are you doing this?" I try not to sound as terrified as I am.

Jake ignores me and continues with the nipple sponge bath.

"He only answers to me. He only obeys my commands." Antonia is sitting in the corner, watching. Her full pale breasts spill out of the top of the leather shelf bustier that exposes her jewel studded nipple ring shields. Her thighs are pierced with ring eyelets which are threaded with round leather laces ending in fringed bows that cascade over her knees. Six-inch stilettos adorn her feet. A riding crop lays in her lap. Her too red lipstick is not out of place now. *What the fuck did we walk into?*

"Then order him to get these fucking handcuffs off me right now!" I might as well speak gibberish for all the headway I'm making. I try a different approach. "Where's my husband?"

"He's in the barn. I'm punishing him for you. You weren't quite up to the task."

"I don't know where the fuck you get off pulling a stunt like this, but when I get out of these cuffs I'm gonna mop this fucking place up with your crippled ass."

"Aren't you mouthy?"

"Bitch, you ain't seen nothing yet." My bravado has not caused Antonia a bit of concern. I struggle against the cuffs that have me tethered to the bed. I only succeed in chafing my wrists and ankles.

"There's no need to be vulgar. I'm here to show you how to handle Simon. He will learn from Jake's example. The rest will be disciplined into him. He shows great promise."

"Are you crazy?" I see the fire in Antonia's eyes. And the alarm in Jake's.

Antonia rolls to the other side of the bed. Jake stops bathing my boob.

"You will respect me." Antonia slaps me across the face with her crop.

I feel the whelp forming on my cheek. *This bitch is crazy. My Spidey senses are tingling out of control. I'm going to have to change my tactics to get Simon and me out of here.*

"Yes, Mistress Antonia," I say, respectfully lowering my gaze just enough to acknowledge her superior position. I hope my words are not betrayed by my rising anger.

"That's better." Antonia eyes me suspiciously. "Your skin is lovely. Do you shave for his pleasure or yours?"

"Mine of course!" This seems like the best response given what I've experienced so far. Truth is Simon has made a sensuous ritual of shaving me – something we both enjoy.

"Good, good. I was beginning to think you aren't serious about controlling your pet. You are fortunate that he realizes his submissive role in the relationship." Antonia pauses, again eyeing me from head to toe. "You strike me as being lenient with corporal punishment," she states, though her tone implies a question that needs my answer.

"Only because I don't want to mar him. That aesthetic doesn't appeal to me." I am determined to play her game as good as necessary to rescue Simon and get us out of here.

Antonia seems to relax a bit. "Sometimes it is necessary. When he is not with you, the scars will remind him he must seek your approval and pleasure above all else."

Knowing how hard it is to get Simon to remember things, I briefly consider this. Tying strings on his fingers and pinning notes in his pockets hasn't improved his memory. Maybe… I reject the thought quickly. This is absurd; this is not me.

You like your body." Another question masked as a statement.

"Yes." Not quite true. I'm not happy with the contour of my butt, though Simon loves it. I file that memory away for another time.

I must focus on getting out of these restraints, finding Simon and escaping this house of horrors.

"You have beautiful skin," Antonia tells me again. She draws the tongue of the riding crop lazily over my mons, teasing me wet. My nipples harden and poke forward. The piercing hasn't short-circuited any nerve endings between north and south. I resist the temptation to fully enjoy the carnal pleasure of the moment. Pleasure I don't want to share with a crazed and crippled dominatrix.

"Very good," Antonia says, witnessing the arousal. "Would you believe I am happy with my body, too? After the accident, when I could no longer walk, I spent months agonizing over my loss. In time, I came to realize that I am also what I haven't loss. I haven't since looked back to who I was. My pleasure comes from who I am."

My thoughts and emotions are all over the chart. I want to ask Antonia how she lost the use of her legs. I shudder at the thought. I don't want to know or understand this woman. She has drugged and mutilated me. God only knows what else. I just want to find Simon and get the hell out of here.

"I need to use the bathroom."

"Simon can be trained to consume your waste, if you wish."

The thought is repulsive, but I know better than to voice my opinion. "In time," I respond, noncommittally. "I need to take care of this now."

Antonia nods to Jake, who unlocks the shackles from my wrists and ankles. He carries me to the adjoining bathroom and deposits me on the ornate chamber chair affixed over the commode. Its height is obviously meant to accommodate Antonia's unassisted transfer from the wheelchair. Jake kneels at the door, head bowed, awaiting his next command.

"I don't hear anything," Antonia says from the next room. "Escape is not possible. Besides, where would you go?"

Escape has crossed my mind. "I'm not used to peeing for an audience," I yell back. Jake's eyes remain downcast. He holds a small mound of toilet paper he has folded onto the palm of his outstretched hand.

I scooch down the bit of lace I'm wearing, release a steady stream and wipe.

"Good to hear," Antonia says.

I wave Jake away as he tries to pick me up for the return trip to the bedroom. I brace myself on the pedestal lav and stare in the mirror. Whatever drugs I've been fed have not worn off completely. I wash and dry my hands. Escape has to be with Simon. I will bide my time.

"Tell me – how're you punishing Simon?" I say, returning to the bedroom and perching on the side of the bed near Antonia. *I can't think of leaving without Simon. If I must bond with this bitch, so be it!*

"He's learning how to subordinate his desire to yours."

Not quite an answer to my question. "What was in that needle?"

"Ecstasy. If you're feeling somewhat disoriented it's probably all the LSD you consumed last night as well."

"I didn't." Then I realize, "the sugar cubes?"

"You did seem to enjoy them. Very much. You appear to have a high tolerance."

Jake is standing over us, holding my fuzzy sweater and boots.

"Slip those on. Let's go out to the barn and check on Simon's progress."

~=~=~=~=~=~=~=~

Outside, Jake maneuvers Antonia's chair down a ramp off the side of the porch. We travel the hundred or so yards between the house and barn along a path of stone pavers. I recognize the barn as one of the buildings silhouetted in the moonlight the night before.

The barn doors open and swing out – responding to the remote-control Antonia operates. My eyes adjust to the dim lighting as I scan the interior space. I gasp when I see Simon.

Simon is seated in a wooden straight-back chair. His legs are duct taped to the chair's legs; his arms stretched behind him, wrapped around the back of the chair, and bound at the wrists with more tape.

His eyelids are taped open. His is transfixed by projected images – a film of the two of us engaged in erotic foreplay. What I don't remember from the night before is memorialized in glorious 5k definition on the giant screen in front of me. Both of us are devouring copious amounts of chocolate sauce off each other.

I turn away from the screen and look at Simon. His imprisoned genitals are a garish shade of purple. Pain and pleasure play across his face.

"He's not going to be much use to me in that condition." I fix a raised eyebrow on Antonia and hope my tone has just enough edge as to not enrage her.

"You're right. The purpose of this little exercise is to teach him control. No matter what he sees or how aroused he becomes, he will suppress those feelings until he is given permission to indulge them."

"Nice theory. It doesn't appear to be working." My causal manner belies my concern. Simon gets aroused watching me take off my mittens. He must be in excruciating pain.

"He will learn," Antonia says confidently.

"Maybe. But I need him right now. Isn't he supposed to be at my beck and call? Well, I want him in my bed nibbling on my clit. Right now!"

Antonia smiles. "Patience. Let me show you some of my favorite toys."

She leads me to a lengthy table. There are so many things: a showcase of plugs and restraints and gags and balls. Clamps and vibrators and paddles and harnesses. Leashes and collars and blindfolds and whips. Ticklers and spiked wheels and lubricants and spreaders. There are all kinds of contraptions on the wall and a basket hanging from the ceiling. A corner of the barn is furnished with an enormous bed under mirrored rafters. My head begins to spin again.

"There's so much," I say to Antonia. I'm truly awed. *Think, Christina. What can you use as a weapon.*

"My collection grows constantly," Antonia says with pride.

I pick up a spreader bar and finger it. Antonia seems pleased with my choice. I move along to examine handcuffs and blindfolds.

"What do you have in mind?"

"This," I say, jabbing her in the chest with enough force to overturn the wheelchair. Before Jake reaches either of us, I aim for his groin and jam the bar into the cage. Jake doubles over, screaming in pain as he topples onto the floor. I almost apologize before I restrain him in a pair of combo cuffs that leave him hog-tied.

Antonia struggles to free herself from the chair. I grab the duct tape from the table. I have the advantage, and begin binding her to the chair.

"You'll pay dearly for this little improvisation," Antonia spews.

"Shut your kinky-ass mouth." I apply duct tape to make it so.

Simon has not moved during my rampage.

Carefully I remove the tape from his eyes, legs and wrists.

"Mistress Toni is not happy," Simon says as I help him to his feet.

"I don't care! We need to get out of here, Simon, before some crazy somebody else decides to join the party."

Simon is all but dead weight, and I am none too steady on my feet, as we head towards freedom. Just as we reach the barn door, I hear the commotion on the other side. I step back, retrieve and grip the spreader bar tightly, ready to defend the ground I've gained.

The doors fly open. I squint at the faces framed in the midday sun. Millicent, her friend Micah, and three others. From their uniforms, the older man appears to be a sheriff; the others – a man and woman – are dressed as paramedics. *Is this real?* No one says anything for the longest.

"Jesus Christ on the cross!" exclaims the man in the sheriff getup. "What the hell is going on here?"

If someone said they saw me standing in a pleasure barn dressed like a porn star, supporting my husband who's wearing only a dog collar and cock cage, while a similarly outfitted and hog-tied man lies on the floor, and a woman in full femdom regalia is duct-taped to a toppled-over wheel chair, I would urge them to stay away from the drugs that had brought on this wacked-out hallucination. But here I am! And this is real!

Millicent's incredulous expression breaks into an embarrassed smirk. "Sorry to interrupt. I thought you were in danger," she says. I see mischief replace the relief in her eyes. "Mother and Father will be relieved to know you weren't abducted by a sect of David Koresh followers."

Then everyone begins talking – except for Antonia whose mouth is still taped shut and Jake who is waiting for permission to speak.

The sheriff – I've convinced myself he is the genuine article – steps further into the barn, looking at our abductors. "Colin? Sarah?"

Micah is taking all this in, almost as amused as Millicent. The two of them wander over to the toy table. They examine the toys. Millicent fondles the Womanizer, while exchanging naughty grins with Micah.

"Anyone care to enlighten us about this little play date?" Micah asks, looking over at a struggling Antonia.

The sheriff and male paramedic quickly set Antonia and wheel chair upright.

"Yes," I say loudly. "We've been drugged and restrained." I lift my sweater. All eyes rivet to my exposed breasts as I point to the bar running horizontally through my left nipple. "I have been pierced against my will."

Millicent breaks out in laughter. "Un-fucking-believable!"

"It's beautiful, Chrissy," Simon slurs as he lavishes wet kisses on my breast.

"Simon!"

"Yes, Chrissy," he grins.

Jake or Colin or Pet or whoever he is, has been released from the restraints. He stumbles awkwardly to his feet. My breasts yield the floor to the submissive hunk in the cock cage.

"You asked for this," Jake states. "How else would we have known your birthstone?" Jake lowers his eyes. "Forgive me, Mistress, for speaking without permission," he addresses Antonia.

The sheriff examines the duct tape binding Antonia. Gently he removes the tape from her mouth. Bruising is evident where I jammed the spreader bar into Antonia. The paramedic with Janice embroidered on her jacket removes a disposable scalpel from her trauma pack and begins to slice through the duct tape binding Antonia to her chair.

For the first time, I notice the ball ends of the rod piercing my nipple. "Diamonds – if they are diamonds and not zirconia – are common gems in jewelry," I state defensively.

Micah's lustful stares earn a poke in the ribs from Millicent. He shrugs it off as I lower my sweater. Its length only serves to accentuate what I'm not wearing.

Paramedic Carl hands me a warming blanket that I quickly wrap around my waist. Carl lifts the sweater back up and examines my piercing. His touch and look are clinical. *How often does he see things like this?*

"It'll heal. Six months, a year – tops. It'll be okay," he professionally reassures me. "If you decide you don't want to keep the piercing, just remove the rod, keep the area clean, and the hole will close up on its own. Do you need something for pain?"

What I need is something to make all of this go away.

"Miss, how did they know it was your birthstone?" the sheriff asks. "You don't deny that is your birthstone, do you, Miss?"

I drop my sweater again to cover myself.

"My husband and I were abducted," I scream. But my words are drowned out by the passionate moans emanating from the giant screen playing last night's sexcapade.

"Nice close up, Christina," Millicent says, as she watches me on screen. "I never knew you were such a chocoholic."

I cover my eyes and squeeze my temples. "What are you even doing here?" I rage at my sister.

"I was worried when you didn't call to say you had arrived safely. I tried calling several times – yours and Simon's phones. The calls went straight to voice mail. I was worried."

"She was, Christina," Micah confirms. "I had a hard time getting her to focus on our playtime." Micah is fingering the Ben Wa balls at the toy table. "She kept imaging you and Simon stuck in a ditch and being tortured by Klansmen and Davidians. "Is that a Chinese basket?" He and his attention drift over to the wicker swing suspended from the rafters.

I ignore Micah. "How did you find us?" I ask Millicent.

"When your phone came on we just followed the find me app," Millicent says. "Micah thought it best to get reinforcements, so we stopped in town to get help. Sheriff Charles was worried something might have happened to the folks out here when he couldn't get hold of anyone. That's why we brought the paramedics. Really, Christina, I was worried. We all were worried."

"I remembered to plug the phones in after the chocolate, before the shower." Simon sounds pleased with himself. "Don't you remember, Chrissy?" he says with a wink.

"Anybody got a key for this thing?" Janice calls out, kneeling before Simon and examining the cage. She is much too close to Simon's penis and testicles for my tastes.

I burst out in hysterical sobs. Immediately, Millicent is comforting me in her arms. "It's gonna be alright," she tells me.

Simon produces a key from a concealed pocket of the dog collar and hands it to Janice. I am dumbfounded.

"You've got a key! Why didn't you take off that god awful thing before now?" I ask.

"Mistress Toni said that only a woman could take it off. And you never asked, Chrissy."

I turn to Sheriff Charles. "Do you need any more proof that we've been drugged?"

"Yes, Miss, I do. Why don't we start from the beginning?"

Again, everyone is talking at once. The sheriff whistles us silent. He turns to the one person who has yet to put in two cents – Antonia.

"Uh, Sarah, why don't we start with you?" Sheriff Charles suggests.

"This man called to arrange a fantasy weekend," Sarah/Antonia says.

All eyes turn to Simon. We wait for Simon's loopy expression to register that an explanation, clarification or denial is expected.

"Simon."

"Yes, Chrissy."

"Did you call Sarah?"

"No."

"Liar," Antonia seethes. "I have the receipt for the money you deposited in my PayPal account."

I try not to be angry. "Simon, did you call Mistress Antonia? Did you put money in her PayPal account?"

"Yes, Chrissy. It was for our special weekend."

"It must be the drugs," Micah whispers to Millicent. "Simon is more absent than usual."

"I take it you don't have this much unintentional drama with all your clients," Micah says to Antonia.

"They are the first couple we've hosted." There is regret in Antonia's voice.

I almost feel her. It's hard getting a small business off the ground.

Micah raises an eyebrow. "Really? Virgins all around. So, when's the next party?"

"Don't even think about it." Millicent emphasizes this with another jab to Micah's ribs.

"Sir, can you tell us what prompted you to engage the Millers for this weekend...get together?" The sheriff's question clearly baffles Simon.

"Focus Simon. Antonia and Jake are Sarah and Colin Miller," I tell Simon.

"OOHH...right."

"Simon, I thought you were planning a getaway at a B & B."

"I was, Chrissy. I did. I saw this ad on a website: 'Want to be the perfect husband? Want to make all her fantasies come true? BD/DS our specialty. Call 555.774.5824'."

This he remembers verbatim!

"What made you think that drugs and body piercing are my fantasy?"

"Remember that talk we had about drugs?"

"No."

"It was Disco Night on the cruise."

"Oh, yeah," I revise my answer. "You remember that, Simon?"

"I do. You wondered what LSD-laced sugar cubes tasted like. Don't you remember? And you said you wouldn't be afraid to do drugs if you were with someone you trusted. And lusted after. We trust each other – don't we Chrissy? I lust after you all the time. Don't you feel the same way? Was I wrong to put LSD and Ecstasy on the list of things to do with you?"

"But Simon…"

"Yes Chrissy."

"I never said I wanted my nipple pierced."

"No, but you said you really liked some of the jewelry and that it's kind of sexy. I think it's sexy too. I thought I'd surprise you."

"This is ridiculous," Antonia asserts. "You could have stopped this fantasy at any time. Why didn't you just say the safe word?"

Simon bites at the corner of his lower lip. "I forgot," he says sheepishly. "I guess I forgot to tell you, too, Chrissy."

"Amazing what Simon's mind remembers and forgets," Micah comments to Millicent.

Sheriff Charles looks around the barn, his scolding gaze pauses on the life-size images of Simon and me in flagrante delicto on the giant screen.

"I'm thinking I've got four consenting adults here," the sheriff says.

"I didn't consent to any of this." My on-screen moans drown out my off-screen protest. I shake my head. I am exhausted. "I just want to go home."

"Go! And take this mindless man with you," Antonia says.

"Algorithm!" Simon shouts. "That's the safe word."

Unbelievable is the unspoken word of the moment as everyone looks at Simon.

"If you ask me, none of you are ready to party and play," Micah says.

"Nobody asked you. And what would you know about it anyway?" Millicent challenges.

"I'm just saying there's no permanent damage. It might be best to chalk this up as a learning experience and walk away." He turns to Antonia, "no malice intended."

"None taken," she smiles back.

This time Micah manages to sidestep Millicent's assault on his ribs.

"Folks, if it's all the same to you, I'd like to close this incident and get back to my office and try to forget what I've seen here. Is anyone pressing charges?" Sheriff Charles asks.

Antonia, Jake, Simon and I shake our heads "no."

"Does anyone need further medical attention?" This from Paramedic Janice.

"No," we say collectively.

"Well, then, I wish you folks well and a safe trip back to Chicago," Sheriff Charles says as he leaves the barn. "Colin, Sarah, I'll see you in church tomorrow. Good day to you all."

~=~=~=~=~=~=~=~=~

An hour later, Simon and I are dressed, and our bags are stowed in the back of Micah's SUV. Simon has paid Antonia and Jake an extra $1000 cash – $300 borrowed from Micah – for our debut video. The local garage has towed our car to the salvage yard.

"Next time I'll be better prepared," Simon announces as we pull out of the yard and turn onto the dirt road leading to the highway.

"I don't think there'll be a next time, Simon," Micah says. I'm pretty sure you're on Antonia's flake list, and those lists get around. She'll probably gain a lot of dom cred warning others about you. That'll be good for her business. Besides, Christina may never want to repeat this fantasy. Am I right, Christina?

"Amen to that," I say. I close my eyes, cuddle up next to Simon, and settle in for the ride home.

"I'm sorry I ruined our weekend, Chrissy. I got it all wrong this time. I promise I'll make it up to you."

"We'll talk about it later."

"So, what do you think?" Micah asks Millicent.

"They'll be fine. Simon and Christina love each other. This is just one small…"

"Not them. And I have my doubts there. I'm talking about the little present I snagged for you from the toy table. Look in my jacket pocket."

"Omigod! It's the Womanizer!" Millicent squeals.

"Souvenir for my baby. Had to recoup something. That video was way over-priced."

"I heard that!" I laugh for the first time since my attack of the giggles at teatime. At least as far as I remember. Simon pulls me closer.

"I love you Chrissy."

"I love you, Simon. I want a divorce."

"Sure, Chrissy. Then we can get back together and break up again. And both end up at the timeshare. Did I tell you I bought the timeshare? Doesn't matter. You'll find out during the property settlement. Anyway, we'll fall in love and get married again. It'll be an excellent adventure!"

I'm too tired to say anything more. One way or another, all will be right with my world.

Think before you speak
Words can wound just like bullets
Both leaving you dead

Pay It Forward

There were just the two of them in the store, minutes before closing, on this sub-zero January night. Memphis watched the old woman judiciously study items before putting them in her shopping cart or returning them to the grocery shelf.

Must suck to be old and broke, having to pinch pennies, he thought. *Probably after years of making sure kith and kin had the best of everything, too.*

As they approached the checkout counter, Memphis stepped aside to let the old woman go first. She put her meager selections on the belt, opened a worn coin purse and extracted a few small denomination bills.

"Fourteen dollars and eighty-seven cents," the clerk said, stifling a yawn. "Paper or plastic?"

"Aren't these items 50% off?" She pointed to the shrink-wrapped meat. "You know, reduced for quick sale?"

"Nope. We don't sell it like that anymore. We just toss it in the morning. You can pick it out of the dumpster for free then."

Memphis recognized the humiliation the clerk's words elicited.

"I'll pay for her," Memphis spoke up.

"No, young man," the old woman shook her head. "I'll just come back later."

"I insist."

Memphis paid for her groceries, bagged them carefully in her cloth shopping bag and watched her leave the store. The "thanks" in her cloudy eyes reinforced his humanity. He needed that.

Memphis turned his attention and his steel revolver to the asshole clerk. "Empty the register. Put it in plastic."

The clerk complied.

Still, Memphis shot him dead before leaving the store.

We are not alone
Our family is boundless
Immeasurable

The Village

Marc Fields opened the front door of his home to a strange silence. No voices. No music. No TV. He did not hear Pooch's heavy paws and trimmed nails on the hardwood floor, running from the family room to greet him. Marc dropped his messenger bag and coat, walking quickly past the family room to the kitchen. He froze, staring at the gun that moved to welcome his arrival.

"Mom!" he shouted, then quieter, "Mom. Helen. It's me, Marc. What..."

His query trailed off as he rounded the kitchen island to reach her. The sight of Gail lying face-up in a pool of blood stopped him. Gail's eyes were wild, disbelieving. Near the open back door, Pooch, their 80-pound Kugsha, lay guard across Shane, the two covered in blood.

Marc took the gun from Helen Thomas and laid it on the countertop. At that moment, all the strength and resolve drained from her body. She collapsed into the comfort of her son-in-law's arms. Marc steadied her and went to his daughter and Pooch. Both were still breathing. Shane was unconscious – a large knot swelling on her gashed forehead. Pooch had a gaping wound on his right flank.

Marc dialed 911 and tried to comprehend the nightmare he was reporting.

Tears streamed down Helen's cheeks. She shook her head and repeated over and over, "she should have stayed away."

~=~=~=~=~=~=~=~

Marc stopped pacing in front of the desk and slammed his fist down on it, jarring everything that wasn't anchored. From the corner of his eye he saw the tank-sized security guard move into position.

"I'm good," he told the guard, holding up both his hands.

"Keep it under control," the guard said sympathetically as he backed off.

"Mr. Fields, this is not an animal hospital. We cannot treat your dog." The receptionist repeated, very slowly, as if Marc didn't understand English.

"Pooch was stabbed while protecting my daughter. And you're telling me that there isn't a doctor in this place capable of treating his wounds?"

"Mr. Fields, this is a people hospital." She emphasized the word 'people', her words heavily peppered with condescension and sarcasm. "You should take your dog to a vet. If it really is a dog," she huffed. "It looks like a wolf to me, and nobody in his right mind is gonna go near it."

"So, tell me what I'm supposed to do," Marc's rising frustration even more ominous in his well-modulated tone. "My daughter is unconscious and our dog is bleeding to death. You don't want to push me!" he warned.

"Marc."

Marc turned at the sound of his name to find Dee Winslow approaching the reception desk. Tall and slender, she walked with a "take charge and no prisoners" attitude.

"I'm Dr. Deidre Winslow," she told the woman at the desk as she flashed her credentials. "Where's the patient?"

"Yes, Doctor." The receptionist snapped to attention and consulted the computer screen. "Shane Fields is in x-ray," she said professionally. "They've just finished up her scans. She'll be back in her room shortly."

"And where is Pooch Fields?"

"You got to be kidding!" the woman scoffed.

"No, I'm not Tonya," Dee said, reading the name off the woman's badge. "I do understand your position. We don't treat animals here." Tonya felt buoyed by this tacit support.

"Obviously, though, you've never had a beloved pet, so you don't understand the bond between this animal and his human family." Tonya's self-righteous smirk faded.

Dee continued, "You're right. Pooch should be in an animal hospital, but since he was brought here, the very least we should do for this canine hero is stabilize him and transport him to an animal hospital where he can get proper care. Anything else would paint this hospital in a very unflattering shade of callousness. And personally," Dee leaned closer as if they were girlfriends having an intimate talk, "I wouldn't wish on you the task of explaining to that little girl that her dog died because he couldn't be treated here. Now where can I find Pooch?"

Shamefaced, Tonya pointed towards a gurney at the end of the hall. "But it mauled a woman," she said, making a final attempt to justify her behavior.

"Thank you," Dee said, ignoring Tonya's last comment. She headed towards Pooch. Marc followed.

Dee steeled herself as she eased back the bloody sheet. "Steady, boy," she spoke softly as Pooch's ears peaked. His soft silver coat was soaked in blood, some areas already stiffening as the blood dried. Dee nuzzled her face close to Pooch's. His breathing was shallow, his eyes narrowly focused, but he managed to push his tongue out of his mouth to lick Dee's cheek.

Dee stroked his head gently. "Hold on, Pooch. You're going to be just fine, boy. And so is Shane. You did your job well. You protected her." Pooch's eyes sparkled briefly at the sound of those words.

Dee straightened and began wheeling the gurney towards the ambulance bay. She spoke rapidly to Marc, who was striding alongside.

"Pooch is disoriented, but not in shock. Doc Murphy's waiting at the clinic. I think all the blood is making it look worse than it actually is," she reassured Marc. "Primary concern is infection, and you've bought us time there. You did good packing the wound. Now go look after your daughter. I've got this."

With that said, she left Marc standing at the bay entrance as the veterinarian ambulance pulled out, lights flashing.

When Marc returned to the ER cubicle where Shane first had been examined, his best friend Jeremy was there waiting.

"They brought Shane back, then moved her up to pediatrics – room 428. Shelia is with her."

"Shelia is here?" Marc questioned. "I thought she was on her way to Springfield for the teacher summit."

"I caught her before she hit I-57. Did you think she would go downstate knowing our goddaughter was hurt? And, yes, I told her. I'm not putting myself in the doghouse 'cause I put off telling her about this. By the way, how's Pooch?"

"Dee came for him. She's in the ambulance with Pooch, heading to Doc Murphy's. Before she left, she schooled that snippy wench at the front desk on how to behave like a human being."

"Pretty smooth moves for a shrink," Jeremy said. "I think she's a keeper," he winked.

Marc looked around the room. Without the huge Hill-Rom bed, there was an eerie ambiance in the space. Shane's blood-stained clothes were lying in a heap by the wall. Sterile packaging and discarded bandages on the floor magnified the feeling.

Jeremy put a comforting hand on his friend's shoulder. "Let's go," he said, steering Marc towards the elevator.

When they reached the fourth floor, they paused briefly to scan the sign across from the elevator, then proceeded in the direction of room 428 at a quickened pace.

Marc moved swiftly to his daughter's side. Shane looked so much smaller than her eight years, even though the bed was youth-sized. Her cut had been stitched and looked less ghastly, but the bruising around her eyes was more prominent now. Her right arm was in a sling. Marc clinched his fist involuntarily at the thought of his little girl in the hands of her crazy ass mother. Calm returned, though, as he glanced at Shelia sitting in a chair beside the bed, her hand protectively covering Shane's.

"I'm Dr. Ruben Shapiro," a man announced to the group as he walked into the room; a middle-aged woman followed. "I'm the attending," he said.

All eyes turned to the doctor. Marc stepped forward, extending his hand, "Marc Fields, Shane's father, and her godparents Jeremy and Shelia Dawson," he said gesturing at his friends. "How's my little girl?" The fear was there in the question.

The doctor's grip on Marc's hand was measured: just enough pressure to covey confidence and authority, but not enough emotion to predict either a catastrophic diagnosis or a rosy prognosis.

"Not to worry," he said, "Shane is fine. She sustained a severe blow to the temple. The trauma caused minimal inter cranial swelling. We've detected no bleeds. Lots of superficial bruising as you can see. We popped her shoulder back in its socket, and there were no tears. The sling is to relieve stress on her shoulder; Shane will need it only for a few days. She's been given a tetanus booster and will be on an antibiotic drip for another hour. Normally we would have discharged from the ER in 2-3 hours; however, we are concerned that she is still unconscious. That's why we've admitted her. We'll monitor her throughout the night, but we anticipate her waking up soon. Sometime tomorrow we'll do a pupillary reaction test to make sure her vision isn't impacted. Again, we don't foresee any problems."

Marc exhaled. He hadn't realized he'd stopped breathing while the doctor spoke.

"I'm sure you'll want to stay the night," Dr. Shapiro continued. "That couch folds out to a bed." He pointed to the pleather sofa under the window.

"I'm Audrey," the woman spoke up. "I'm the pediatric nurse assigned to Shane for this shift. If you need anything or have questions, just ring the call button here." She pointed to one of the several buttons on the bed's side rail. "I'll have housekeeping bring some fresh linens down for you."

"Thank you. Doctor. Audrey," Marc, addressed the pair, nodding to each as he spoke.

No sooner had they left, then Dante and Simone Fitzgerald came into the room. Dante was the third member of the triad. Marc, Jeremy and Dante had been together since day one, freshman year at St. Chad of Mercia. Theirs was a twenty-year friendship.

Both Dante and Simone were lawyers: Dante in private practice and Simone with the ACLU. Marc had called Dante after he called the police. The fact that they were here, without Helen, alarmed him.

The first words Dante said to Marc were, "It's okay. Helen's fine."

"I convinced Helen to stay the night at her friend Edna Connors'. She's exhausted – running on adrenaline and about to crash," Simone supplied answers for the questions she knew Marc must be thinking. "You know she'll be here first thing in the morning. Nothing will keep her away. But right now, she needs as good of a night's rest as she can get."

Marc nodded his agreement. "Thanks, you guys. I couldn't bear the thought of her spending the night in jail. Or alone."

"I know man. You gotta know, though, it was this feisty little mouthpiece who did most of the work," Dante said proudly of his wife. "She may be five-foot nothing, but when she starts talking, they all stop and listen."

"The restraining order you took out on Gail and the other documented incidents definitely factored favorably into the decision," Simone added. "The police will still need to talk to Shane. Dante and I will be there for her – and you – when that happens.

A young man from housekeeping knocked as he entered, carrying sheets, blankets and pillows. He looked at the crowd and asked, "Should I get another foldout and more bedding?"

"No," Jeremy said to the young man, then to Marc, "we're clearing out of here so you can get some rest. It's been a long night."

"I can't thank you enough," Marc began, looking at his best friends and their wives.

"No need to. We have each other's back. It's what we do," Dante said.

The five exchanged hugs and kisses. Then Marc was left alone. While the sofa was being transformed into a bed, Marc's phone vibrated. The message was from Dee: "41 stitches. No major organs damaged. Pooch resting well. See you in the morning."

Marc closed his eyes, relieved. He appreciated Dee. She was no nonsense, no drama. Shane liked her, too. And Dee understood them. *Yeah, she was a keeper.*

The guy from housekeeping was gone. Marc lowered the lights and kicked off his shoes. He ignored the pull of the freshly made bed, opting instead to settle in the recliner since it was closer to Shane. He pressed the speed dial number on his phone to connect to Helen. He skipped his mother-in-law's recorded greeting and went directly to voicemail to leave a message.

"Hi, Mom. Rest easy. Shane and Pooch are both doing fine. I'll see you in the morning. Mom." He hesitated before speaking the next words. "I'm sorry about Gail, Mom. I really am. I love you."

Shane stirred in the bed. Her beautiful brown eyes, her mother's eyes without the craziness, struggled to focus in the dimly lit, unfamiliar room.

"Daddy!" she cried out.

"Right here Shane," Marc answered. He moved to the bed and enfolded his daughter in his arms.

At his touch, the words flowed nonstop from Shane. "It was awful Daddy. I didn't want to go with her. I was so scared. I was yelling for Grandma. Mother kept shaking me and yelling me to shut up. Pooch was barking and trying to get in his door, but it was latched. And then Mother slapped me really really hard and I fell and hit my head on the counter. I tried to stand up. I kept falling down. Mother was dragging me to the back door. She opened the door and Pooch ran in and jumped on her and knocked her down. He was biting her and she was screaming. She got away and grabbed the knife. She was cursing and stabbing at Pooch."

Shane looked around the room. Tears were pooling in her eyes. The rapid fired words were replaced with a fierce demand. "Where's Pooch?"

"Shane, honey, Pooch is at Doc Murphy's clinic. He got cut badly and lost a lot of blood. He had to get a lot of stitches. Pooch is gonna be fine. He won't be doing any running and playing for a while, though."

"I'll take good care of him Daddy," Shane said, already planning Pooch's convalescence. "I won't let Pooch walk. I'll read to him. I'll bring everything to him. His food and water. Should we get him a litter box like Mercy has for Snowball?"

"We'll see what Doc Murphy recommends," Marc smiled.

"Daddy, can I sleep with you tonight?" Shane asked, trying not to sound like a baby.

"Sure, honey."

Marc moved the IV pole and its infusion pump to the other side of the bed. He carefully lifted Shane from the bed and carried her to the recliner and sat down. He made sure all the connected tubes weren't tangled and her arm remained tucked protectively in the sling. He covered them both with the lighter of the two blankets, then reclined the chair.

Shane snuggled against Marc. "Good night, Daddy."

"Good night, Shane." Both were sound asleep within minutes, but not before Marc silently thanked God that Shane hadn't seen her grandmother shoot her mother.

~=~=~=~=~=~

Sometime during the night another pediatric nurse came in to check on Shane and introduce himself. He suggested that each might be more comfortable in their own bed, but didn't insist on either one of them moving. He took Shane's vitals and disconnected the IV. Shane slept peacefully in Marc's lap through the procedure.

~=~=~=~=~=~

Hours later, Marc woke to the aroma of dark brewed Ethiopian coffee and chocolate. Dee was arranging pastries, coffee and cocoa on the bed tray.

Shane woke, rubbing her eyes and wincing at the pain.

"Let's get Shane back in bed," Dee told Marc.

Marc raised an eyebrow, but did as instructed. Behind her, from the other side of the room, Dee wheeled a gurney next to Shane's bed. "I need a little help, Marc," she said. On the gurney was a portable kennel and Pooch was in it.

"Pooch! Pooch!" Shane squealed with glee, her free arm outstretched.

"We have to be very careful not to jostle Pooch too much," Dee told Shane. "He's going to be very sore for a long while."

Shane nodded. "I'm sore too, Miss Dee. We can be sore together."

Marc helped Dee lift Pooch, who was lying on a quilted pad, onto the bed.

"Thank you, Miss Dee," Shane said, cozying next to Pooch.

"Thank you, Dee," Marc echoed. "For everything. Especially last night."

"It's what friends do," Dee smiled.

"Aren't we breaking some hospital rule here?" he asked.

"Bending is more like it. Shane and Pooch are the best medicine for each other. Trust me. I'm a psychiatrist. I know these things. Besides, I'm currying Pooch's favor. If I ever have to face a mob of apocalyptic zombies, or a crowd of Walmart Black Friday shoppers for that matter, I want Pooch by my side."

Just then, Helen Thomas hurried into the room. Her eyes revealed more anguish than any parent should have to bear. Marc tenderly embraced Helen, then hugged her tighter and whispered, "thank you," against her neck.

When he released her, Helen went straight to her granddaughter. She kissed Shane's forehead, recoiling slightly at the injuries her daughter had inflicted on this precious child.

Pooch opened wary eyes, assessed no imminent danger and closed his eyes again.

Shane looked at her grandmother. "Hi Grandma. We're sore and we're resting." She closed her eyes. And snuggled closer to Pooch.

"Party's in here," Jeremy called out as he, Shelia, Dante and Simone came into the room. They had balloons and other gifts for Shane. Jeremy carried a stuffed dog nearly as large as Pooch under his arm. He stopped short upon seeing Pooch lying protectively next to Shane. "There's no substitute for the real thing," he said tossing the giant stuffed animal in the corner.

Every face in the room lit up watching Shane and Pooch cuddled together.

Marc reveled in the unconditional love and support filling the room. There was Dee stepping up to be where he couldn't be, and Jeremy and Shelia dropping everything to be there with him, and Dante and Simone taking charge of Helen's welfare. There was Helen who killed her daughter to protect his. And there was Pooch, intelligent and bred to work, always protecting this family.

And then the raw pent-up emotions overtook him, and Marc knew he could no longer contain them. He quickly, quietly moved to the hall. His silent tears turned to audible sobs that racked his body. Jeremy and Dante flanked him. The women, in turn, surrounded the men in a group hug.

As capable as he was, he was blessed not to face life alone. It meant that Shane would always belong somewhere. Marc thanked God for his village.

Frugal versus cheap
One is the best management
One is controlling

A Penny Saved

Elizabeth hated it when Ronald went to the grocery store with her. He scrutinized everything she put in the cart. After fifty-five years of marriage it was one of many idiosyncrasies she had grown accustomed to, if not fully endorsed. But this latest offshoot was a step too far. For whatever reason, Ronald felt compelled to enlighten others with his unsolicited advice.

Elizabeth, face flushed with embarrassment, watched as Ronald explained to a young woman why organic produce was a scam. The cornered young woman was trying to retreat graciously, smiling and nodding as she backed herself and her cart away from Ronald, but he persisted, following her into the adjacent bakery department, where he switched his monologue to the outrageous markup for "some baked flour, water, salt and yeast."

Elizabeth grabbed an expensive bunch of asparagus, and went to the young woman's rescue. "How about this for tonight's dinner?" she asked as she approached the two.

Upon seeing the asparagus, Ronald immediately abandoned his bread lecture and stared at his wife. Aghast, he said, "Have you lost your mind, woman? Under the best conditions it's overpriced, but asparagus is out of season and that bunch is organic." Ronald shook his head as he took the vegetable back to its display. "Elizabeth, I don't know what's gotten into you. If it weren't for me you would spend us into the poorhouse."

No chance of that, Elizabeth thought. *Not on a food budget of $50 a month.*

"We have to watch our pennies, so that we have enough to live out our golden years in comfort. We can't depend on the government or Christian charity to see us through old age," Ronald said.

Elizabeth hardly felt she was living out her golden years in comfort. Everything was a battle with Ronald. It was not just how money was spent. He measured the toilet paper on the roll, chastising her if too much had been used since his last daily inventory. He separated the raisins from the bran flakes in the cereal to determine the exact number to redistribute in each 60-gram bowl. Just once she would like to wash dishes with as much suds as she liked instead of the paltry amount produced from the Ronald-prescribed one teaspoonful of dishwashing liquid. His behavior was no longer frugal, it was downright miserly.

"Are you listening to me Elizabeth?"

The question brought Elizabeth back to the present. "Yes, dear," she said, steering the cart towards then end of the produce section. "Let's look at the discount rack. I'm sure there'll be something not too bruised or over-ripe that will suffice."

"That's my girl," Ronald said, beaming as he followed Elizabeth towards the shrink-wrapped bargain produce.

~=~=~=~=~=~

Twenty minutes later, reusable shopping bag in hand – which he had reminded the clerk to give him full credit for, Ronald and Elizabeth left the grocery store to walk the four blocks home. As courtly as ever, Ronald extended his free arm to Elizabeth as they began their stroll.

Approaching the corner, Ronald sped up as the red flashing hand heralded the changing of the signal light. Elizabeth would have preferred to wait for the next full light, but she increased her pace to keep up with Ronald, holding tighter to his arm.

As they reached the opposite curb, Ronald handed the grocery bag to Elizabeth. Mesmerized by the glint of a copper penny, Ronald stepped back off the curb to retrieve it. Just as he straightened up and was about to remark on his good fortune, a cargo van racing to make the turn before the light turned red slammed into Ronald, propelling him several feet forward and upward, into the rear windshield of a parked car. Ronald rolled off the car and onto the pavement with a bone-cracking thud.

~=~=~=~=~=~

Elizabeth didn't know how much time had passed. She sat on the curb in a daze. There was a flurry of activity: ambulance paramedics working on Ronald, police officers taking statements from witnesses, the young driver sobbing that he'd looked away "for only a second" and "the old guy just appeared out of nowhere."

When all was said and done, Ronald was driven off in the ambulance, without the urgency of lights and siren, and Elizabeth was driven home in a squad car. At her front door, the officer handed Elizabeth the grocery bag and a manila envelope containing Ronald's wallet, keys and watch. "I'm very sorry for your loss, Ma'am," the officer said as Elizabeth let herself in. She nodded and shut the door between them.

Elizabeth carried the groceries to the kitchen, staring vacantly as she walked through the house. *What will I do without Ronald?* He had been her life since she was twenty-three years old. And it had been a good life for the most part.

The doorbell rang. Elizabeth waited, expecting to hear Ronald yell out, "I'll get it. I wonder who that could be." Then she realized she would never hear Ronald say those words again. Elizabeth would have to answer the door herself.

Elizabeth opened the door to find her next-door neighbor standing on the stoop. Gloria rushed in, enveloping Elizabeth in a consoling hug. "I just heard about Ronald. I'm so sorry. What can I do?"

"Nothing," Elizabeth said flatly, "I'm fine."

Gloria stepped back across the threshold. "If there's anything you need, just call over. The kids can go to the store for you."

Elizabeth smiled a forlorn "thank you" as she closed the door. Suddenly she jerked it open. "Gloria, if it's not too much trouble, I have a taste for some Ciao Bella mango sorbet." Elizabeth had never had it before; it had always been an unsatisfied indulgence.

"No problem," Gloria said. "I'll send the kids right now. And don't worry about paying me. It's the least I can do."

Elizabeth shut the door again, a smile teasing at the corners of her mouth. Perhaps she did know what she would do without Ronald.

First kiss promises
No matter how old we are
Take our breath away

First Kiss

He'd seen her before on several occasions – at events hosted by local civic organizations and at charity fundraisers. He'd always nodded and she would smile in return. But now he dared himself not to behave like a tongued-tied teenager and more like the successful retiree that he was.

He waited until she was alone, then strategically placed himself in her line of vision. When she noticed him and smiled, he crossed the room to greet her.

"Good evening," he said. He extended his hand. "Andrew Montgomery." *Damn! Did that sound too formal?*

"I know," she said, letting her hand slip into his. "I'm Faith Bridges." Faith found herself giddy within. She was flattered that this handsome man sought her company when there were several young women less than half her age vying for his attention.

She had seen Andrew at other events, and he had appeared hesitant to engage in anything beyond a polite acknowledgement. She wasn't surprised. Women her age were burdened by so many ridiculous and negative stereotypes, while their male cohorts were not similarly branded.

She smiled again and Andrew was lost in her chestnut brown eyes. He realized he was still holding her hand. *How lame is this?* Thinking quickly, he shifted his position, tucked her hand around his arm and said, "Come look at the Kirkland seascapes with me."

"I'd like that."

They moved through several gallery rooms, arm in arm, making their way to the room where the series of Doug Kirkland seascapes were prominently displayed.

They took in each of the vibrant oil on canvass paintings, moving from one to the next in silence. When they had viewed them all, they found a seat in front of a huge oblong piece entitled *Windswept*. They sat close to one another caught up in the ferocious white capped dark waves.

Their silence was not uncomfortable for either of them, but each felt the need to break it.

"It reminds me of..." Faith began, just as Andrew said, "when I was a boy..."

They both laughed.

"You first, Faith," he said.

"It reminds me of an Alaskan cruise I took with my parents some years ago. It was late in the season, mid-September, and the Inside Passage was unusually choppy. That first night out more than half the passengers and a third of the crew were seasick. I suppose being tossed about on such a large ship made it worse. The captain changed course to salvage the voyage. Mom, Dad and I were among those who loved the motion. We sat on deck in slickers and life jackets, exhilarated by the giant waves washing on board." Faith touched her cheek. "I can feel the spray on my face when I look at this painting." She smiled at the memory.

Had she said too much? Andrew was staring, the look on his face indecipherable.

"What about you, Andrew? How does this piece speak to you?"

Andrew cleared his throat. "When I was a boy, on those brutally cold winter days, I used to watch the waters rise up out of Lake Michigan and freeze in midair. It made the most beautiful ice sculptures." He was still staring.

"Was that here in Chicago?"

"Yes. I was born and raised here – Englewood, Hyde Park, Edgewater. I'm settled in Hyde Park now. I've been many places in my fifty-eight years, even lived abroad a few years courtesy of Uncle Sam, but Chicago is always home for me."

"I grew up just north of the city – in Evanston; I've lived there most of my life," Faith shared. "I moved to Hyde Park four years ago."

There was that smile again. Andrew liked this woman. She was at ease with herself. By and large he'd learned over the years that women who weren't obsessed with age, wrinkles and pounds, were far more intriguing.

"Would you excuse me for just a moment?" he asked, pulling his phone from his pocket. "I have to attend to something."

"Of course," Faith replied. She hoped he'd return – that she hadn't scared him off.

Andrew found a quiet alcove and texted the gallery owner. While waiting for an answer, a young woman approached. Early twenties, he guessed, and dressed to display her bountiful assets. She planted herself in front of him. Not his cup of tea.

"It's like so refreshing to see a man being like so nice to his mother," she gushed.

Strike one. Cheap snipe. No reasonable person could ever mistake Faith for my mother. Andrew doubted Faith Bridges was forty-five.

Andrew moved to step around her. She blocked his escape saying, "I'm Elantra." She winked mischievously and added, "My mom like named me after the car I was conceived in."

Strike two. TMI as the tweeters would say. He wondered if her approach ever worked. Probably not for long, since she seemed to be on the prowl.

Elantra placed an outrageously manicured hand on his forearm and said, "Like do you think we could get a drink? It's like so hot in here." Elantra punctuated this last comment with a lick of her lips.

Strike three. Inappropriate and excessive use of the word like.

Andrew had no interest in becoming this siren's buy-toy. "Please excuse me. I need to get back to my mother," he said.

Elantra pouted, but was soon off in a flash, having eyed another potential benefactor.

Andrew wove through the crowd to the bar, secured beverages and made his way back to Faith. She wasn't there. He looked around the room, in a panic, until he finally located her standing in front of a quartet of miniatures.

Relieved, Andrew sighed as he watched her. He liked what he saw. He liked the sparkling strands of silver hair mingled in the deep brown. Faith had a graceful posture, exquisite movement. The tailored slacks and camisole sweater set she wore complimented her toned body. She was as much a work of art as any of the pieces in the gallery.

When he reached her side, he offered her one of the fluted glasses. "Ginger beer," he said.

"Thank you." Faith took the glass and smiled. *He must think I'm dense. Say something witty!*

Andrew's phone chimed.

Ah, saved by the ringtone. "Do you need to take that?" Faith gestured to the phone in his pocket.

Andrew took it out of his pocket and looked at the screen. "No. Just a confirmation I was expecting."

They enjoyed each other's company the remainder of the evening. Winding through the rooms, they talked about many things beside their fondness of art.

Andrew learned that Faith was a schoolteacher, but only worked substitute assignments since moving to Hyde Park. Like him, she'd never married, but her life was not void of adventure. He liked that about her. Unlike him, she had never played golf, though she enjoyed hiking. They both loved fishing, though neither had been recently. Yoga and tai chi maintained Faith's inner and outer balance. He preferred swimming. She was an avid reader, and like him, loved all forms of literature. Each claimed *Empire* as a guilty pleasure.

Andrew wanted to know more about Faith, and was disappointed when the gallery began to close. He asked for her phone number.

"You have an iPhone," she said. "I'll airdrop you my contact information."

Faith showed him how the feature worked, and within seconds her image was smiling at him in his contacts, complete with name, number and email. He was impressed. He quickly created a contact of himself and airdropped it to Faith.

"Did you walk, drive or taxi here?" he asked, as they stood on the sidewalk in front of the now dark art gallery.

"I drove," she replied. "My car is just around the block."

They walked to the corner and turned. Halfway down the street, Faith stopped.

"This is me."

Her car was a classic khaki-colored 2005 Jeep Grand Cherokee with a 5.7L hemi. It was outfitted with heavy duty off-road tires, stub antenna, grill and bumper guards and fender flares. There was a hitch for hauling and reinforced roof racks. Trail rated, it was well suited for off-road trips.

Andrew's thoughts drifted. The thought of a weekend fishing trip crossed his mind. Imagining the two of them, snug in a sleeping bag under the stars, bristled the hairs at the nape of his neck.

Andrew admired the near perfect body – he saw only a couple of dimples to the finish. Faith took good care of this car. "I like these older models," he finally said. "They're solid and dependable. You've maintained it well," he complimented.

"She's the last new car I bought. It was a 40th birthday present to myself," Faith said. "I call her Blondie."

Andrew quickly calculated. *Faith is fifty-two! I never would have guessed.*

Andrew seized the moment as they stood by the driver's door. He kissed her chastely on the mouth, his lips lingering on hers for more than a few seconds. He felt her lips smile through the kiss. This woman could warm his heart as well as his bed.

He stepped back as Faith turned off the alarm and she got into her car.

"Wait here," he instructed. "I'll get my car and follow you home. That way I'll know you arrived safely."

"If you like," Faith said.

He nodded. *Appropriate use of the word like.*

Andrew followed Faith's car, driving to an Ellis Avenue address. He watched her park Blondie and enter a three-flat building one door down. The second-floor lights came on just as his phone rang.

"Thank you for a lovely evening Andrew. Call me when you get in, so that I know you arrived safely. Good night for now."

As he drove home, Andrew felt like a boy; his hormones were raging. He replayed the kiss over and over in his mind, savoring the sensations it ignited. He anticipated a lot more kissing, and then a whole lot more of a whole lot more.

He thought about *Windswept.* He hadn't been sure when he impulsively texted the offer, $200 over the asking price, to the gallery owner. Now he was. He would give the painting to Faith on their one-month anniversary, the anniversary of their first kiss. And if all went well, within the year, *Windswept* would hang in their bedroom.

Reluctant hero
He knows what it means to serve
Now's his chance to live

Face Value

The handwritten thank you notes had appeared out of nowhere – just like the uncharacteristically warm spring-like days that February.

Monica recalled the first one:

> *To the Unheralded Soldier,*
> *I can't imagine my life without you.*
> *Thank you.*

That was the beginning of a weekly ritual. Each Monday – for 41 weeks now – among the many pieces of mail that arrived at the inner-city VA clinic was the five by four-inch envelope. It was not addressed to anyone, just the clinic in general, and there was no return address. Each was postmarked on the preceding Saturday from a random suburban postal facility.

The folded note inside was of a heavy ghost white card stock – the kind which is usually embossed with the owner's initials. This stationary, however, bore no such crest. Anonymously, the sable textured card was beautifully calligraphed with an earnest message of gratitude.

The tribute that arrived today read:

To the Unheralded Soldier,
I will honor your selflessness by
not living my life selfishly.
Thank you.

After the fourth note arrived Monica created a special board in the waiting room to display the notes. With each addition, the speculation increased. Monica reasoned, because the sender had chosen to be anonymous, that the spotlight was intended to fall on the veterans that came to the clinic. Still, no one could resist wondering about the sender.

Including Monica. She was not immune to the mystery. Over the months, she had constructed several intriguing profiles. She had finally narrowed it down to her two favorites: a war widow who wanted to acknowledge the ultimate sacrifice her husband and many others had made; and a father, himself a veteran, whose son or daughter was beyond earthly thanks.

"Good morning Harry," Monica said as the younger of the clinic's two doctors walked into the general staff office.

"Good morning, Monica."

Dr. Harrison Cook, distant and detached, had worked at the clinic for over a year. He remained an enigma. Monica knew from his curriculum vitae that he was a Cornell graduate, had attended St. George University Medical School and had completed his surgical residency at Mayo Clinic.

She suspected that even though his education was impressive, there must be some scandalous deed in his past. This theory was bolstered by a three-year gap on his vitae, which neither she nor other office staff could fill in with information gleaned from polite queries and casual conversations.

Whatever had happened, it was a career buster. Why else would he bury himself in such a dead-end job? Doctors with far less impressive credentials than Harry had come and gone from the VA clinic – staying only long enough to leverage themselves into a more profitable and prestigious position.

Today, as Monica had noticed on several occasions before, a barely perceptible tremor shook Harry's hand as he reached for a patient chart. She wondered if his hand had shaken during a procedure. Was he recovering from a crippling malpractice lawsuit? That would explain why he ate peanut butter and jelly sandwiches at his desk every day. He just couldn't afford to eat out.

Even so, whatever his past sin, Dr. Harrison Cook appeared to have a unique bond with his patients. No one ever complained – no matter how long they had to wait to see him. Monica wondered what connected him with his patients and at the same time distanced him from the staff.

"Hey, Monica," Stephanie Jones, one of the patient assistants greeted her. "How was your weekend?"

Before Monica could reply, Stephanie spied the note card and squealed, "We got another one! What does it say?" Again, she didn't wait for an answer, taking the card from Monica's hand and reading it for herself.

When she finished, she sighed, "I could so fall in love with this man. He's just so sensitive and romantic."

Monica saw the disinterested look on Harry's face as he left the room.

"What makes you think the sender is a man – and a young man at that?" Monica was curious. She had rejected that profile almost immediately. The average guy just wasn't that in tune with his feelings.

"I just feel it. He's young – twenty-five or so – tortured by an epic loss. Like a twin brother who went to war without him and never came home."

"We've got patients, ladies," Nurse Cynthia Thorne, said, poking her head into the office. "Let's follow that example," she pointed to the note card, "and serve our veterans well."

~=~=~=~=~=~=~=~

"Good night, Harry," Monica said.

It was 6 o'clock on Friday evening – the end of a long and exhausting week. Monica had finished filing the last of the updated patient charts, and was heading out the door.

"Good night, Monica." Harry hadn't looked up, from reading the current issue of JAMA. He sensed her hesitation at leaving him alone. "I'm not staying much longer. I want to finish this article first and write a few notes."

"Have a good weekend then."

"You, too."

Harry listened for the slide of the deadbolt lock. Alone, he began to knead the muscles in his cramped fingers and hand. Fortunately, Monica hadn't noticed the forefinger of his right hand stiffen and extend to a thirty-degree angle.

As his muscles relaxed, Harry, thought of Paraguay and the People's Militia. Harry did a few repetitions of hand-flexing exercises until nothing remained except the numbness in his ring and pinky fingers. And the memory of the months spent in the keep of the enemy.

Using the desk chair, Harry rolled over to the corner and retrieved his backpack. Back at the desk, he unzipped one of the smaller compartments and took out a note card and envelope, a calligraphy pen and ink.

He laid everything out, with surgical precision, before taking pen in hand and dipping it into the ink. Carefully he touched pen to paper and made the first stroke. He willed his hand to behave.

When his orthopedic surgeon had suggested he incorporate calligraphy in his physical therapy routine – as a way of gaining control over his movements – he had balked at the idea. Now he saw the value in it. The intricacies of the pen strokes required that he hold his pen at a certain angle, that he apply and release pressure at a precise moment, that he move the pen between ink and paper cleanly and efficiently. It was not unlike the relationship among hand, scalpel and body.

Harry had completed writing the salutation when he heard the noise at the door. Quickly he covered the note card with the copy of JAMA. He turned to see Monica standing in the doorway.

"I didn't mean to interrupt," Monica apologized. "My car won't start. I was hoping you could give me a jump. I've got cables," she added awkwardly.

"Sure," Harry said, grabbing his coat. He wondered how long Monica had been standing there – if she had seen what he was doing.

Of all the women working in the clinic, Monica was the most appealing to him. It wasn't because she was pretty or because she was closest to him in age, though those two factors didn't diminish his attraction. It was because she possessed a genuine empathy that put everyone at ease and made it hard not to like her. And he liked her.

Right now, he felt trapped. Should he bring up what Monica may or may not have seen, or be silent?

Out in the parking lot behind the clinic, Harry got in his car, started the engine and popped the hood. Monica's car, which was parked next to his, already had the hood up. Harry connected the two cars' batteries and signaled Monica to start her engine. One false start, and then Monica's engine revved to life.

"Better let it run for a few minutes," Harry instructed, leaning into Monica's open passenger side window.

"You should get in out of the cold," Monica offered him the seat beside her.

Harry got in and Monica rolled up the window. Both said nothing. They stared straight ahead. The wiper blades came on, intermittently swooshing the fine icy mist from the windshield.

"It's you," Monica said, after what seemed an eternity of silence.

"Yes." Harry had thought about a conversation like this each time someone had speculated about the author of the notes. He hadn't foreseen it happening like this.

The silence now was oppressive. Monica regretted her intrusion. She respected Harry's privacy, and knowing him as she did, she knew she'd stepped over the line. She knew what she had witnessed. She hadn't needed his confirmation.

"The engine should be good now," Harry said.

They both exited her car. Harry turned off his engine. He detached the cables from the batteries and handed them to Monica. He slammed both car hoods shut.

"Thank you, Harry."

"No problem."

Monica watched Harry walk back to the clinic.

Harry paused just before opening the door and looked back at Monica. She was still standing there. Watching him.

It's you. Those two little words echoed in his mind. They stood ready to unburden his tortured soul. *It's you.* Those two little words spoken by anyone else could never carry so much weight. *It's you* mattered because it's her – Monica.

Harry retraced his steps to her.

"If you have the time, Monica, we should talk."

Monic nodded. She stowed the cables in the trunk, turned off the engine, and followed Harry into the clinic.

Once inside, their outer coats shed, Monica said, "Harry, please forgive me for prying. I have no right. Whatever I saw remains between us."

"I appreciate that." Harry thought about his next words. "Monica."

"Yes, Harry."

He motioned for her to sit down in the straight-back chair beside the desk.

"I want to tell you something. About me."

"You don't have to."

"I want to."

Monica sat. Harry seated himself in the desk chair. Harry's posture changed several times as he gathered his thoughts into words.

"Are you familiar with La Milícia del Pueblo – The People's Militia?"

"No."

"La Milícia. – they're freedom fighters – protesting the inhuman and constricting powers of the established government in rural Paraguay. They organized around 2005. I was in Paraguay in 2008, working with a non-profit, non-partisan group of doctors on a humanitarian mission when our paths crossed." Harry spoke quickly, racing to get the words out before he lost his courage.

"In those days, La Milícia funded their activities by kidnapping and ransoming wealthy tourists. One of their hostages became seriously ill. I was kidnapped to treat her, which I did. When the ransom was paid for her, I was not released. It was seven months later that I was left in the mountains for the government's army to find me." Harry exhaled deeply – eager to continue his story, yet apprehensive to bare suppressed emotions.

Monica wanted to ask questions. *Were these the missing years? How long was he alone in the mountains? Did those terrorists injure his hand?* But she said nothing. She waited.

"When I was with La Milícia, I cared for the wounded soldiers and treated the peasants they brought to me. I was el médico – the doctor. My role was apolitical. I was respected as a healer, and that's all I did. I was left behind when my presence was more of a problem than a benefit."

"It must have been a relief to be rescued by the government."

"No." Again Harry's posture shifted as he gathered his thoughts. "The regional government treated me like a terrorist, a conspirator. I was jailed and interrogated. I was tortured. My hand was accidently broken – twice. Each time I was denied medical treatment."

"Oh, my God, Harry! How could they treat you that way?"

"They believed I knew more about my kidnappers than I had told them. They believed that justified their actions."

The words of the chief jailer still haunted Harry. *"You are the big shot American doctor aiding the rebels and their sympathizers. Fix it yourself!"*

"Oh, Harry. How horribly unjust. What made them finally come to their senses?"

"They never did."

Monica tilted her head slightly to the right. "I don't understand."

"I was to be executed as an enemy of the government." Harry's eyes closed, the pain obvious.

Monica recognized the pain on Harry's face as being more than a remembered trauma. She saw the spasms take control of his right hand, contorting his fingers. His expression confirmed the excruciating pain traveling along the neural pathways to imprint on his brain.

She got up and went to the adjacent exam room, returning with a disposable heat pack, a towel and a small jar containing coconut oil mixed with frankincense and cypress essential oils. Monica sat facing Harry, the towel on her lap, and before he could object she placed his hand on the towel. She opened the jar and took out a small amount of the salve to massage into his hand.

"You don't have to, Monica. I'm fine."

"I want to. I know you're fine, but your hand could use the attention."

As Monica massaged the fragrant oil into his hand, Harry shut out everything but her touch. The warmth and strength of her fingers expertly soothed his rebellious hand, bringing a relief that even his physical therapist hadn't achieved. It felt too good. He withdrew his hand. She took it back. He gave in.

"I was going to be executed," he said. "The doctors I had been traveling with, who had been searching for me since my kidnapping, had been expelled from the country. My family fought for my return to no avail. Our government was mired in diplomacy, red tape and outright lies. Towards the end, for the first time in my life, I knew what it was to be expendable – an unfortunate casualty. And then I was rescued.

"I knew they couldn't abandon you! Was it the Marines? Black Ops?"

"No. I was rescued by the same rebels who had kidnapped me."

Monica was stunned. "The rebels?"

"Yes. That day, I was blindfolded – wrists bound behind me – standing in the prison yard, shaking and praying death would be quick. I had seen others before the firing squad. They were shot with enough bullets to maim and torture, then left to die from septic shock.

"I knew the guards were lined up in front of me – I had seen them when I was led out of the jail. I heard the chief jailer give the command. I heard the guns click, followed by silence, then rounds being fired amid shouts and running.

"By this time, I had dropped to my knees, and was now lying face down in the dirt. I don't think I breathed the few minutes it all unfolded. The next thing I heard was the rebel leader say, 'Help the good friend doctor up.'"

Monica was still massaging Harry's hand, though she herself hadn't breathed while he recounted the ordeal. "The rebels killed those soldiers to rescue you?"

"Yes. They had thought I would be safe with the regional government. After all, I am an American." Monica heard the tinge of hurt and bitterness in those words. "The rebels thought that by leaving me behind, I would be out of danger as the regional government's army pursued them. When they learned of my fate, they returned to right the injustice they had set in motion."

"How did they do it? You said you heard the clicking of the guns. Why didn't they fire?"

"The girl who serviced the soldiers was a member of La Milícia. She removed the firing pins."

Harry saw the troubled look on Monica's face at the mention of the girl and her lot in life.

"That girl, her sisters and mother were raped by government soldiers; her brothers and father murdered. She was twelve when they destroyed her life – her innocence. Her younger sister went mad; their mother took care of her best as she could. Her older sister killed herself. That young girl, Chava, was resilient. She turned her body into a weapon to use against her defilers. I owe her my life."

Monica was overwhelmed with rage and sadness. She shook her head. *So much suffering and heartache. And for what? No doubt, greed and power were at the root of this evil.*

"I assume the rebels got you safely to the American Embassy and didn't leave you alone to fend for yourself again."

"They tried. But I had become a liability. The murder of my jailers was a political quagmire. I was not welcomed home."

Harry... no," Monica shook her head.

"I roamed with the rebels, I hid among the peasants. I repaid their kindnesses with what I had left of my skills. It was almost two years before I was smuggled out of Paraguay. And again, it was the rebels who facilitated my fate. I quietly reclaimed my life four years ago. My time In Paraguay is forgotten by the powerbrokers here and there."

"All that time, Harry. Lost. Away from family and friends. Forced to do the bidding of the enemy. I can't imagine surviving what you have."

"It wasn't easy, Monica. I did learn a lot about myself and human nature in those years. I came to know the face of the enemy well. It is fear. I rarely saw it in the eyes of the rebels. It was always there in the eyes of the authorities, consuming them with the need to stop everyone else from having what they believed was an exclusive right to some resource or power."

"I don't understand. Weren't you afraid?"

"Oh, yes! My fears were of dying, of being forgotten, of never operating again. Some days I wallowed in those fears. Fear was my true enemy – not the rebels, not the authorities. And when I replaced fear with hope, I understood. The rebels' actions, my actions, took on a different meaning."

Monica considered how fear chips away at the spirit and facilitates defeat. She encountered it with her patients. She had experienced it herself. She nodded. She understood.

Monica reached for the hot pack and activated it before Harry could object. She wrapped it and his hand in the towel, keeping all three in her lap.

Harry cleared his throat. The proximity and the heat triggered emotions he wanted to explore – just not yet.

"I've kept you long enough, Monica. You needn't stay any longer."

Monica felt it, too. She rested her hand on top of the towel. "I have no plans, Harry. I don't mind staying."

For the next thirty minutes, Harry and Monica talked about less weightier subjects – what each liked to read, favorite television shows – old and new. They discovered they were Trekkies – each favoring Picard, but irresistibly drawn to Kirk since his younger years had graced the big screen.

When the heat pack began to cool, Monica unwrapped Harry's hand. He flexed his fingers, pleased with the result.

"Maybe I should change physical therapists," he complimented.

"Maybe you should," Monica said, indulging in a bit of 'the doctor and the therapist fantasy'. "Not that your therapist isn't doing a fine job," she quickly added. "Calligraphy is an excellent rehabilitative tool."

"About those notes."

"You don't have to explain anything more, Harry."

"The rebel leader, Cristóvão Mirante. He died February 8th from sepsis. The notes are my way of remembering him, honoring him."

Monica nodded again. She understood. So much, now.

Harry glanced at the clock on the wall. It was close to eight o'clock. The last two hours should have been exhausting, but he felt exhilarated. He didn't want that feeling to end.

"How about we grab some dinner? My treat," he suggested.

"No, Harry. I don't want you to go to the expense."

Harry weighed her words carefully before saying, "It's no big deal, Monica. No strings attached."

"That's not what I meant, Harry." Hesitantly she added, "it's just that you always brown bag your lunch. And it's always peanut butter and jelly."

Harry grinned. "And you think I'm strapped for cash." The grin became a hearty chuckle. "I'm not living paycheck to paycheck, Monica. I can afford dinner," he assured her. "I just like peanut butter and jelly. It was the one thing I craved while I was away."

Monica blushed at the misperception. "Dinner sounds good, Harry. Your choice. I'll follow you in my car."

They locked up the clinic and got in their respective cars. Again, Monica's car wouldn't start.

Harry was at her door as she opened it. "Looks like I'm riding with you," Monica told him.

"Not a problem," he smiled. "Not at all."

My life immortal
I wish it were different
It's hard being god

Time Changer

Back in 2020, a young scientist, Travis Roberts, found a way to genetically determine life spans. Like most major discoveries, the pie-eyed liberals saw its application as a benefit: if one knew how long they had to live, one would maximize their potential.

The reality of it was that people, being people, found a way to subvert any benefit right out of the equation. Some chose to live it up, breaking every law and social norm, knowing they would never live long enough to pay for their crimes. Others saw it as a license to apathy: what did it matter, why even try, since the damn sword was hanging over your head?

The weirdest thing was that the "expiration" date was immutable. At least that's what I believed back then. Neither accident nor willful act could change it. That was very depressing for the suicidal. But you know what they say – never underestimate the entrepreneurial spirit.

Enter California showman/producer Peter Allen. He developed a reality show, *Death Challenge*, where suicides would attempt death in some sensationally bizarre way. If you succeeded, you got what you wanted and were the dead winner. If you failed, you got to live in a chemical coma for the rest of your predicted life. *Death*

Challenge consistently garners 25 million viewers each week. And in eight seasons, in uniquely orchestrated pop up locations around the country, there has never been a winner – not the chainsaw battling twins, or the chef who deep-fried himself, or the gal who slit her veins and has been bleeding out for the last four seasons. All their tickers just keep on pumping as they live out their life in medically induced coma at the Suicide Hospice Museum, founded and funded by viewers like you.

But I digress...

A bunch of offshoot industries sprang up as well. The most commercially successful was GenoMark. Those geniuses found a way to date stamp a fetus in the womb. Now every bouncing baby can emerge from the womb with their expiration date clearly tattooed on their bottom right heel. And for those wishing to be on the cutting edge of technology, après-birth tagging is available through independent genetic labs.

Which brings me to my kind. Not the ones born pre GenoMark, though maybe that has something to do with it. The others like me – I can sense them, even though I've never met one of my kindred – are immortal. We have no fixed expiration date.

Let me tell you a bit more about me – then you decide. I was born in 1953 – long before lifespan prediction and in utero tagging. I was fast approaching seventy, and had just retired from my forty-year career as a pension actuary, when all the hoopla was in high gear. I hadn't given it much thought before, but now I wanted to know just how much time I had left to complete my bucket list.

According to the little stick I peed on – I used an OTC digital lifespan test – I had two years left. Well, you do the math: I took the test on my 70th birthday in 2023; I should have died in 2025 - eight years ago – yet I'm still here. The manufacturers of the lifespan test I took, boasted a 99% accuracy rate, so I decided not to opt in for a more detailed analysis and tagging from the lab. I had two years left, and I intended to make the most of them.

Okay, I know what you're thinking. Nothing I've said so far points to immortality. On the contrary, if anything, my life appears to be mundane and mortal. But before you dismiss my claim to immortality as an old man's wistful delusions, predicated on a faulty test, let me explain how I came to this conclusion.

As I said, I had two years. I had dreamed of going to Africa when I was a teenager. My friend, Emil, had joined the Peace Corps after we graduated high school, and had been living in Africa ever since. He became a doctor, running a clinic in Gwakwani.

I booked passage to South Africa, and emailed my friend to expect me. By the way, Gwakwani literally translates to armpit. Gwakwani was a forgotten community in the age of technology. Hell, they didn't have electricity until 2014! When Emil brought me to the village I was surprised at how quickly it had caught up. Gwakwani was as modern as any north shore Chicago suburb. Only costume and culture identified it as different.

During the day, I spent my time exploring the village and the surrounding areas. Late afternoon, I found myself at the clinic waiting for Emil to finish seeing his patients and join me for our evening meal.

I had noticed there was a woman with a young boy in the clinic every day. Emil told me the boy was expiring in a little more than six months, and the mother kept coming to him, hoping for a cure.

It saddened me to watch her. One afternoon, after observing her fruitless vigil for more than a week, I offered her the only thing I could – comfort. I moved over to the chair next to her and touched the woman's hand; her son stood leaning against me, fascinated by the second hand sweeping around the face of my wrist watch.

"It is unfair that my life will not end for another fifty years. My son is only six. He should have my time," she told me.

No sooner had she spoken those words, then she slumped over in the chair. Emil was unable to revive her. Her heart had simply stopped. The boy, now an orphan, was placed in the care of his mother's sister.

The following week, the aunt brought the boy to the clinic. When Emil examined the boy, his tattoo showed an expiration date thirty-eight years into the future. Those who knew of the boy and his mother could talk of nothing else. Emil and I puzzled over this for days. Had the mother somehow managed to transfer her remaining lifespan to her son? And why only seventy-five percent of it? In the end, the anomaly became a miracle and no one looked for further explanation.

Weeks later, on my return flight home to Chicago, I still pondered this miracle. The universe offered no answer, though a clue from an unexpected source did present itself. As I entered the lobby of my apartment building, the doorman greeted me with, "ya lookin' real fit, Sir. 'Tirement 'grees wit ya."

Upstairs in my bedroom, I examined my face closely in the mirror. I did look more relaxed – ten years younger, even. I had attributed it to the absence of the daily work grind. *Could it be twelve-and-a-half years?* The thought pushed into my mind unexpectedly. That would be exactly twenty-five percent of fifty.

I rushed to the pharmacy for a lifespan test. The results supported the conjecture: another twelve and a half years had been added to my life. But how? I revisited the events of that day in the clinic. Nothing stood out. Whatever had happened, I was blessed with another twelve and a half years. Who looks a gift horse in the mouth?

I went about establishing a routine befitting my retirement and extended life span. I did things I'd never made time for: museums, art galleries, fishing, weekend trips. I indulged in new rituals like taking coffee at the corner cafe.

On that definitive day, I had just finished my mocha latte, which I had spiked with bourbon from my pocket flask, and was walking back to my apartment. A young woman zoomed by me on a bicycle. As she crossed the alley, a truck moving at breakneck speed slammed into her, crushing her beneath the massive rear tandem wheels. I reached her as the driver exited the cab and staggered towards us. Dropping to my knees, I supported her mangled body in my lap. "Not now. Not like this," she pleaded. Her voice was barely a whisper.

"You asshole!" I screamed for her. "What were you thinking, backing down an alley like that? Look what you've done! Help her!"

The truck driver took in the carnage, then callously yanked off her shoe. "No point wasting a Band-Aid bus on her. Today's her day."

I grabbed his arm as he started to leave. I looked at him with an intense hatred and disgust the likes of which I had never felt before. If looks could kill...

And then he dropped dead. Just like that. And the young woman rallied. Just like that. She pulled herself up off the ground. A bit dazed, she braced herself against the alley wall. As she put on her shoe, a glimpse of her heel revealed an expiration date forty-five years into the future. I inched away from the dead trucker, not sure of what to think or do as a crowd gathered around the scene.

"Just goes to show you. When it's your time it's your time," I heard someone comment.

"Yeah," came the reply. "That accident should've taken her – not him."

My heart pounded in my chest; I could not make sense out of what was happening. Effortlessly I stood and ran. I ran all the way back to my apartment, not at the pace of a seventy-one-year-old arthritic man, but of one decades younger and more agile. I slipped in the back entrance of my building, avoiding the doorman and fellow tenants.

Ensconced in my apartment, I paced back and forth, unable to quiet the adrenaline rush. In the den, I channeled my energy into a chart on the chalkboard wall, listing the variables in each incident, calculating percentages. When I had finished and stood back to examine my data, I saw the pattern.

I was a conduit, a transmitter. In each incident, I had been a physical bridge between two people. In each incident, a wish or desire had been expressed – one with which I had total empathy. In the first incident, I had received a twenty-five percent commission for my services, or so it seemed. If this theory was correct, the next stick I peed on should show fifteen more years had been added to my life.

I sat down at my desk and pondered the implications. Was this really happening? How far could this age regression go before I was no longer an adult? Could I empathize myself right out of existence? And why me? No one would ever accuse me of being a warm and fuzzy, touchy-feely kind of guy. I am the left-brain poster child. Could the same process – executed in reverse – age me beyond my actual years? Would that subtract years from my expiration date? And more importantly, what could trigger that?

You are not alone.

I swiveled around in my chair to see who had entered my den. No one was there. I got up and walked around the room, looking behind the door and drapes, then ridiculously extending the search to places too small to conceal a person. I found no one.

I must be going mad. That was the only logical explanation. My situation analysis was flawed. That's all there was to it. I sat down again and swiveled my chair to face the chalkboard wall. I pulled out my cell phone and snapped a picture of the wall, then flipped to the forward-facing camera. The face I had shaved that morning, with its puffy eye bags, cloudy corneas, crow's feet and slack jowls, was not looking back. This was the forty-something me staring back. Was it possible I could live forever?

Yes.

That damn voice again! I knew I was alone in the room. Maybe... I didn't know any longer. I closed my eyes, cleared my mind. And then I felt them for the first time. I felt their energy. Others. Just like me. I felt their consciousness. I needed to know more.

There is no rush. We have all the time in the world.

~=~=~=~=~=~=~=~

That was nine years ago. Today is October 28, 2033. It is my eightieth birthday. I've added a total of fifty-two years to my life span; I look and feel thirty. For all intents and purposes, I am immortal. I possess an immortality that is both blessing and curse. I have enjoyed a youth I did not fully appreciate and live before. I have agonized over the lives I've saved and the ones I haven't. It's not easy being a god.

I am learning how to live with immortality day by day. I have no guidebook. I have no mentor. Occasionally I hear another, usually in response to my desperate loneliness. Occasionally I respond to the lonely laments of another.

I've moved often to protect my secret.

With added life comes many regrets. Emil, the one friend I would have shared my secret and gifted with added life, died seven years ago. It was his time and I was not there. Even I have no control over the weather and commercial flights. And if I had been there, who would I have taken life away from to give to him?

I am learning the rules as I go. I know that I cannot create an immortal being like myself. I cannot wish someone a long healthy life and change their expiration date. If I had that power, I would marry – wisely – and be content for the rest of my existence.

At times, I have felt unbelievable joy. Did the others feel this when I first came into my power? I also have felt an overwhelming emptiness and loss. I wonder if that marks the end of one of my kindred. That would mean all of us – my kind and yours, alike – only live once. But how long is that for me? I am impatient to know what I am, why I am.

The only answer I hear is *soon*.

Guarding heart with head
Think you missed living life
May be a good thing

Cecelia

Cecelia did not trust people who were nice to her. Too often she had been on the receiving end of someone's self-serving or mischievous deed.

Her earliest humiliation was in junior high, when a girlfriend helped her write a letter to the boy of her dreams. Cecelia had poured her heart out in that letter, only to witness her girlfriend read it aloud to a group of cool kids in the school cafeteria. At the time, her mother had told her how treacherous girlfriends could be, and warned Cecelia that girlfriends were only loyal when it was to their advantage.

"More often than not, girlfriends are just out to get your man," her mother advised.

Cecelia felt so close to her mother as they talked about relationships. Her mother kept her out of school the rest of the week, and their quality time was like a dream come true.

That Friday, Cecelia's mother let her cook her favorite foods: zucchini appetizers, smothered short ribs, glazed carrots, asparagus, scalloped potatoes, and an exquisite chocolate cheesecake with strawberry sauce. Cecelia loved cooking; she was comfortable and relaxed in the kitchen. When she had finished, she proudly admired the results of her efforts. Her mother was equally pleased; she set the table for two with her best linens, china, crystal and flatware.

As it turned out, it was just another betrayal.

"When Jimmy gets here, you can serve us and excuse yourself," her mother casually announced. "You can watch TV in your room. Or call one of your little girlfriends and sleepover."

A regrettable college love affair and a promotion derailed by a scheming office mate further convinced Cecelia that she was one of those people that everyone claimed to like and admire, but didn't hesitate to shaft if it were in their own best interest. Since she did not believe true friendship was within her grasp, and she had no desire to keep her enemies close, Cecelia resigned herself to life on the periphery – observing life from a guarded and safe distance.

And then came Harold.

"What're you doing this weekend?" Harold asked.

Harold Cleveland stopped by her cubicle and asked Cecelia Lake this question every Friday for the last five-and-a-half months.

"Washing my hair, doing the laundry, catching up on my reading, trying out a new recipe." This was always Cecelia's reply.

"There's the Clark Street Festival this weekend, if you're interested. I know one of the bands playing. It should be a great show. The weather is supposed to be sunny and in the 70s. What do you say?"

"Thank you for asking, but no."

"Maybe another time. If you change your mind ... you still have my number?"

Cecelia smiled politely. "Yes," she said, turning her attention back to the computer screen and ending the conversation. Harold self-consciously walked over to the break room.

Why does he continue to ask me out? Cecelia wondered. She would never accept his invitation. Not because there was something horribly wrong with him. On the contrary, from what Cecelia knew of him, Harold seemed to be a perfectly fine individual. He was liked among their co-workers. He was always the first to support candy drives and fundraising campaigns. And he certainly was physically attractive.

Harold's face was perfectly symmetrical, his eyes were a pale cool gray and his nose was neither broad nor delicate – it was just right. He had a wonderful smile and an amazing mane of shoulder length caramel blond hair culminating in a widow's peak that framed his face when it was not tied back in a ponytail. Standing six feet, with broad shoulders and muscular arms and legs, Harold was very pleasant to look at.

Which caused Cecelia to wonder why such a nice and attractive guy would be interested in her.

Not that Cecelia thought herself without a certain beauty of her own: her weight was in proportion to her five-foot-five frame, her figure was unencumbered with excess body fat and her curves garnered both appreciative and envious glances. Cecelia's nails, skin and hair had a healthy glow, and she was often asked about her beauty regimen. Side-by-side, she and Harold would make a beautiful couple.

But what does Harold see in me? What's the catch? Experience had taught her that she was a magnet for manipulators and self-serving losers. Harold appeared too good to be true.

"You know he's going to get tired of the rejection and move on." This unsolicited advice came from Eden Matthews who occupied the cubicle across from Cecelia.

Cecelia didn't respond. She distrusted Eden. Welcoming her to the office, Eden was too eager to befriend her. Her first days on the job, Eden made several attempts to get Cecelia to eat lunch with her. Cecelia always declined, eating her brown bagged lunch at her desk, or citing errands to run. Cecelia was an expert at keeping women like Eden at arms' length.

"Honestly Cecelia, how can you resist Harold? He's just so yummy."

"I'm on a diet," Cecelia retorted.

Later that afternoon, as she was leaving for the day, Cecelia saw Harold and Eden with their heads together, deep in conversation. Cecelia felt oddly satisfied that she had been able to call it before seeing it.

~=~=~=~=~=~=~=~

Over the next week Cecelia observed several hushed conversations between Harold and Eden – conversations which abruptly ended when they noticed her noticing them. Away from Harold, Eden was her usual over-bubbly self, initiating conversations about seemingly innocuous things, solely to extract personal details from Cecelia. With the postured stealth of a private investigator, Eden queried her about favorites: colors, flowers, movies, restaurants. *What was that about? What was Eden's agenda?*

When Harold stopped by her desk on Friday morning, Cecelia did not expect him to ask, "So, do you have any plans for the weekend?"

She found herself disappointed in Harold. Harold had never impressed her as a player, trifling with her affections while openly pursuing Eden. Yet here he stood, his eyes looking directly into hers, falsely exuding sincerity. He and Eden probably would have a good laugh about it later. Cecelia was even more disappointed in herself that she cared.

"Washing my hair, doing the laundry, catching up on my reading, trying out a new recipe," Cecelia recited. She muttered an "excuse me" and brushed past him, heading towards the refuge of the washroom.

Minutes later when she emerged from the washroom and headed back to her desk, Cecelia saw that Harold was still there. He was sitting in Cecelia's chair which he had rolled over to Eden's desk to talk with her.

As Cecelia approached them, Harold stood and moved the chair back to Cecelia's desk.

"Are you ok?" he asked.

"I'm fine." Cecelia added, "Just a little frog in my throat."

Harold was about to say something, but thought better of it. Instead he smiled and headed back to his cubicle.

At the end of the day, Cecelia watched Harold board the elevator. She was glad he had not tried to continue their earlier conversation. She tidied her desk, took her purse from the bottom drawer of the file cabinet and headed to the washroom. No sooner had she crossed the threshold, then Eden pushed in behind her.

"What is the matter with you?" There was anger in Eden's tone.

Cecelia responded with silence.

Eden went on, "if you don't like Harold, even as a friend, you should tell him. Men are dense and they can't or won't read the signs."

"I like Harold just fine," Cecelia lied. A week ago, she had liked him a lot, but the blossoming relationship between Harold and Eden had soured that feeling.

"You don't act like it," Eden accused.

"What does it matter to you? Why do you care?"

"Last week Harold pleaded with me to find a way for him to impress you. I'm such a romantic! I agreed to find out what you like. Harold is really sweet. I just wanted to help. I thought I was being a friend. But now I see that you're not worth the effort. You are too involved with you to care about anyone else. You'll just end up hurting a really nice guy."

Dumbfounded, Cecelia looked at Eden. *How could anyone think that of her?* And then it hit Cecelia like the proverbial ton of bricks. *Could I have been wrong about Harold? And Eden?* Cecelia had called it like she was used to seeing it – injecting past pains into the present situation, never considering another possibility.

Eden continued defensively, "Harold is probably going to make some lame grand gesture, and my guess is that it will not impress you. Look, I don't know if it's that you don't like him or men in general, but he really likes you. Whatever your problem is, please try not to humiliate him."

With that said, Eden left Cecelia alone in the washroom. Cecelia looked at her reflection in the mirror above the wash basin. Eden's words danced in her head, darting among the mantras that had nurtured her mistrust all these years. *What should I do? What can I do? How could either of them expect me to be any different than who I am just because they want more from me?*

Cecelia closed her eyes and breathed deeply. When she opened them, she had regained her composure. She touched up her lip gloss and quickly left to take the elevator downstairs, eager to put the unsettling confrontation behind her. And, of course, because Cecelia wanted to escape her thoughts and this place, she was forced to endure the cell phone-fixated silence of the several passengers collected on the sixteen-floor descent to the lobby. *Where were the excited chatter of strangers and Muzak when you needed it?*

When the elevator doors finally slid open in the lobby, Harold was standing there, slightly to the right, a single stem of yellow calla lily in hand. It was neither her favorite flower nor color.

"Have a good weekend, Cecelia. I hope you feel better."

Cecelia took the flower Harold offered. "Thank you," she said.

Harold hesitated a moment, hoping that Cecelia had more to say. After what seemed an enormous amount of time, he awkwardly smiled and said, "Well, see you on Monday."

Cecelia watched Harold walk away. A voice screamed in her head, *Say something!* But Cecelia was paralyzed with fear. She crossed the lobby and exited the building through the revolving door onto the street.

On the bus ride home, Cecelia thought of nothing else but how she had misinterpreted the relationship between Harold and Eden. *Is it possible that Harold is really interested in me? Just me? Dare I hope to have someone as special as Harold in my life?* By the time she let herself into her studio apartment, Cecelia had convinced herself to call Harold and arrange to meet up.

~=~=~=~=~=~=~=~

Harold listened to the recorded message for the third time, his face radiating happiness.

> "Hi Harold. This is Cecelia. I apologize for being so abrupt earlier today. I just wasn't myself. Well, I was being myself, just that...well... Anyway, the reason I called is to thank you again for the flower. And if you still want to do something this weekend, maybe we could go to a movie or get coffee. But you don't drink coffee...we could have tea or soda. Maybe something at Oberweis. I guess we can decide later. Anyway, I just called to say if you don't have any plans, I can postpone catching up on my reading. Bye now. Oh, this is Cecelia. Did I say that already? Anyway, my number is 5 5 5 6 3 4 5 7 8 9. Bye."

Harold put the cell phone on the side table, and turned to the young woman who had been his house guest for the last few months. Her mind struggled to make sense of Harold's sudden change in attitude.

She really knew nothing about him, but he had been so disarming with his clumsy pickup line, that she had fallen in lust with him instantly. And she hadn't been wrong. At first. It had been fun playing the role of Lady Cecelia to his Sir Harold. The sex had been epic, and she hadn't minded that he never called her by her own name.

But over the weeks – or was it months – the role playing had become more sinister. The drugs and bondage Harold introduced to their games frightened her. And her current role of Cecelia the Stuck-up Cunt, naked and duck tapped to a chair, was not one she enjoyed.

She watched Harold as he moved around the room, tidying up what was already tidy. Harold went into the kitchen and returned with a large butcher knife. *Good*, she thought. The last time he had just ripped the tape off. That bit of pain she could do without. As he approached, she wondered what new pleasure he had in mind once she was free.

Harold flashed his deceptively charming smile and told her, "How fortunate for you. I no longer need your company."

Once there was a dream
Better left unfulfilled
To bring happiness

The Cake Best Left Uneaten

Once upon a time in a city much like the one we live in, a boy met the girl of his dreams. As with most epic love stories, their paths were star-crossed. Too young to own their love when they first met, time and circumstance would continue to keep them apart. Years would pass, each living a rich full life, yet haunted by the dream of what might have been if those magical summer kisses had never ended.

Tonight, the stars will rewind and realign to favor their ardent wish.

~=~=~=~=~=~=~=~=~

REMIX
Labor Day Weekend, 1969

Belinda hurried around the kitchen, quickly packing the picnic basket with all of Jim's favorite foods. They had been dating all summer, and this was officially their third-month anniversary. As she went to the dining room hutch to retrieve her grandmother's hand-embroidered tablecloth, she heard snippets of her parents' conversation carrying from the living room.

"...too serious...the draft...," her father was saying.

"...school...give up her dreams...," her mother responded.

Belinda wished she could hear everything they were saying, then decided she was glad she couldn't. It was probably the same old arguments: she and Jim were too young to be so serious; if Jim didn't get caught up in the draft, he would be miles away at Morehouse; Belinda had high school to finish, and would be going to Howard in a year.

The doorbell rang, and Belinda heard her father's footsteps echoing on the hardwood floor. She heard muffled voices, and then Jim popped into the dining room.

"Hey, Lindy," he said, giving her a quick hug. "Are you ready?"

"Yeah. Just have to get the cake," Belinda said, heading to the kitchen.

Jim followed. His eyes widened as he watched Belinda take an eight-inch square carrot cake from the refrigerator. Carrot cake was Jim's favorite desert. Belinda placed it in the basket, and handed it to Jim.

"What else is in here?" he asked, judging the weight of the basket.

"Just some fried chicken and potato salad," she beamed. Belinda handed him a thermos, saying "sweet tea," to his unasked question.

"Let's get this picnic started," he said.

Belinda smiled and yelled, "Bye Mom, Dad," as she and Jim slipped out the back door.

~=~=~=~=~=~=~=~

Belinda and Jim made their picnic on the Point, a popular spot for young couples. They spread Jim's blanket on a tree-shaded spot that provided a romantic view of the lake rushing the limestone blocks. Belinda spread her grandmother's small round tablecloth at one corner, then laid the scrumptious meal on it. After filling up on chicken, potato salad and sweet tea, they lazed on the blanket, talking between kisses.

"We should always have picnics like this," Jim said. "Even after we've been married for ten years and have five kids, I want to have picnics just like this – just you and me."

"Five kids!" Belinda sat up and stared at Jim.

"That's not so many. I have five sisters and three brothers, you know. I promise you, I'll be there for our family. I won't knock you up and run with the fellas. I'll be a good husband and father, just like my dad was."

The note of sadness in his voice reminded Belinda of Jim's recent loss. His father, who seemed to be in excellent health, died from a brain aneurysm. Belinda touched his hand. She didn't know the words to ease his grief. Instead she said, "How about we start with one? And then a trip to Paris after the baby is born."

"And that is how we will end up having five children in six years, Lindy. All those romantic second honeymoons." His voice was playful, tempting.

Belinda blushed. She and Jim had done little more than kiss, and now they were talking about having sex and babies – in a roundabout way.

"Right now, I'm happy with a slice of carrot cake and a kiss," Jim said, deflecting the tension and sealing the bargain with a kiss.

~=~=~=~=~=~=~=~

June 1971

Belinda sat on the side of the bed. The TV table stacked high with open books threatened to topple over as Jim's wheelchair collided with it.

Belinda tried not to feel annoyed at this purposeful gesture. She knew Jim was angry with her, and this was one of the ways he expressed his anger. She could hardly blame him; she knew he suffered.

This was far from the life they had dreamed of. Her unexpected pregnancy, had caused him to drop out of school to marry her and take a job. Belinda miscarried the baby, leaving them both grief stricken. Then Jim was drafted and sent to Vietnam, only to be shipped home a few months later minus his legs.

Their life together was miserable. Jim resented Belinda for going back to school; he resented the time she was at work. Exhausted all the time, Belinda found herself feeling guilty and constantly apologizing for trying to make a better future for them. Jim's dependence on street drugs didn't help matters. He was slipping away from her, and she felt helpless to make it right.

Money was the only thing they talked about these days. What little money Belinda managed to save, Jim spent on heroin. And now he had proposed this insane solution to their financial woes.

"Are you okay?" Belinda asked, watching Jim rub the back of his neck. "I could give you a massage," she offered.

"How do you think I feel, Lindy?" His tone was caustic. "I can't even stand up and piss like a man! ...I ask one little favor of you and you go off the deep end."

"Listen to yourself," Belinda shouted. "You're asking me to sleep with some guy to pay off your drug debt!"

"Look Lindy it's not like you'd be cheating or anything." Jim cunningly gauged her reaction. Her phony faithfulness really pissed him off. He was pretty sure she was getting some somewhere, since she sure as hell wasn't getting it from him. Probably one of those geeks in her study group. He was way past caring if she had a fuck buddy. All the comfort he needed came from that magical white powder.

"This is business," he emphasized, "a fair exchange. Look if I don't get them the money, they'll kill me!" He waited to see if this would sway the argument. When Belinda said nothing, he added, "course my life isn't worth much to you anyway. It'll save you the trouble of leaving me. And the cost of a divorce."

"It's prostitution, Jim! How could you want that for me?" Belinda's heart was beyond broken. "I can ask my parents for the money," Belinda suggested, almost begging him to consider the alternative she knew he would reject.

"Can they get me five thousand dollars in an hour?" Jim ignored Belinda's shocked expression as the magnitude of his debt sank in. Jim answered his own question. "No! Right? Besides, money from them would give them something else to lord over me. No thanks! They hate me enough already."

"They don't hate you, Jim. They just want to see you better."

"Well there is no better for me! This is it, Lindy. I'm in this fuckin' chair. I'm in constant pain. The only relief I get is from the H." Jim saw this line of reasoning was going nowhere, and Lobo and Chickie would be there soon.

The knock on the door startled them both. Neither moved to answer it.

The knock came louder punctuated by a chilling, "We know you in there Jimbo."

Jim wheeled around and opened the door.

"Nice of you to invite us over," Lobo said, pushing past him into the room. Chickie was right at his heels, closing the door behind them. "Hope you don't mind us dropping by early."

"No. No. Everything's cool."

"This must be the lovely Lindy," he said turning to Belinda. He took her hand and ceremoniously kissed it.

Belinda snatched her hand away and moved closer to Jim.

"No need to be that way," Lobo admonished. "Jimbo here is okay with letting you settle his debt. But first you, me and Chickie gonna get real friendly – see if you worth the marker. If we like what we taste, I'll introduce you to some quality gentlemen." He winked as he moved closer to Belinda.

"No," Belinda said forcefully. Naively she had thought Jim had been coaxing her into a one-time deal. She now knew that was not his intent.

The slap surprised her, propelling her against the TV table, knocking her books to the floor.

"I wasn't asking." Lobo's voice was smooth, menacing, barely above a whisper.

Belinda looked at Jim, silently imploring him to defend her, to stop this madness. Jim's indifference was worse than the slap. His eyes livened only when Chickie dropped a foil square in his lap.

"A little bonus for you," he smirked, "on the house."

Jim rolled over to the card table and shakily began preparing his lifeline.

Lobo grinned at the chaos he caused. Turning to Belinda he promised, "Don't worry doll. We ain't gonna wear out that sweet little pussy of yours. Chickie here is a back-door man."

Belinda tried to maneuver around them, to get to the door and escape. Chickie grabbed her and clamped a hand over her mouth. Lobo stood in front of her and ripped her shirt and bra off. Her struggling only increased Chickie's grip and the hardness in his groin. She felt her shorts and panties being yanked down to her ankles. Chickie set her down, then he and Lobo shoved her back and forth between them, touching her breasts and grabbing at her privates, making disgusting sounds and fouler comments as each unzipped his pants. She was dizzied from the unbalanced motion and fear. Now exposed, Lobo and Chickie held her between them. Belinda cried out in agony as both men entered her at once.

Lobo sneered over his shoulder, "c'mon Jimbo. Three holes, no waitin'."

Jim looked up from his drugged haze to see Belinda suspended between the two gyrating men. Her violation and tears meant nothing. She was nothing – just another fuck doll. Jim wished he'd never married her. She ruined his life.

Through excruciating pain and devastating sorrow, Belinda saw the contemptuous look on Jim's face. What love there had been between them was gone. Belinda wished they had never shared a kiss and a carrot cake.

~=~=~=~=~=~=~=~

And now the stars will shift once more to give back to Belinda and Jim the life they were always meant to have. This time without regrets or reservations.

KISMET
Labor Day Weekend, 1969

Upstairs in her bedroom, Belinda heard the doorbell ring, and her father's footsteps echoing on the hardwood floor as he went to answer it. She heard muffled voices, and then Jim's voice at the bottom of the stairs.

"Hey, Lindy. Sorry you're not well enough for our picnic."

The disappointment in Jim's voice made her feel even worse. She wanted to give him this special day, to take his mind off the sudden loss of his father. All week she had dreamed of their picnic on the Point. They had kissed only twice over the summer, but each time had been magical. There would be none of that magic today.

Belinda came out of her bedroom and stood at the top of the stairs. "I'm so sorry," she said. Her throat was so sore, her voice barely reached Jim's ears.

Jim felt helpless to ease her obvious suffering. "Just get better. I'll call you later," he told Belinda. He said goodbye to her father and was out the door in a flash.

Belinda rushed back to her room as her mother emerged from the kitchen carrying a mug of warm tea.

Upstairs in Belinda's bedroom her mother asked, "why the tears?"

"I'll never see him again. He's leaving for Morehouse the day after tomorrow." Belinda's voice was a hoarse, raspy squeak.

Belinda's father sat on the side of the bed. "He said he would call," he consoled her.

When Jim called the following day, her mother told him that Belinda's summer cold was strep throat, and that had progressed to scarlet fever. Belinda was hospitalized.

Jim left for Morehouse without seeing Belinda again. They talked on the phone – actually, Jim talked and Belinda painfully responded in monosyllables. They made plans for the coming months amid a wistful goodbye.

Belinda recovered, but wasn't well enough to go to Atlanta for Morehouse's homecoming festivities. Finals prevented Jim from coming home for Belinda's winter prom, and Belinda was away on a week-long campus tour of Howard when Jim came home during winter break. Letters and phone calls became less frequent, and as so often happens in life, Jim and Belinda drifted apart. New friendships and experiences faded the memory of their sweet summer romance.

Belinda finished high school and went on to undergrad and graduate studies at Howard. Her business acumen positioned her as a highly sought after thought leader in her field of theoretical economics.

Jim completed his undergraduate work at Morehouse and graduate work at Harvard Medical School. His research contributions were so valued that he received educational deferments throughout the draft.

Both Belinda and Jim thrived. The two would-be lovers never reconnected.

~=~=~=~=~=~=~=~=~

June 2016

Belinda beamed as she walked into the banquet hall on Rodney's arm. Twenty-five years ago, she had all but given up on ever marrying and having children. But when she had least expected it, when she had nearly given up hope, Rodney came into her life, and marriage and four children followed.

Twenty-five years together, and never a moment of regret. Tonight, she and Rodney would celebrate with their families and friends a marriage that was truly destined in the stars.

And half a continent away, on a quiet tree-lined street Jim watched as Marie picked the ripe strawberries from the upside-down contraption they were growing in. His wife truly had a green thumb. Every possible space – inside and outside – hosted plants, herbs, fruits, vegetables and flowers.

Jim held the screen door for Marie as she stepped into the kitchen, her apron full of berries. She unfolded them into the sink, then reached above the sink to pluck some mint leaves from the window sill planter. The love of his life – his grad school sweetheart – making his favorite pie. Jim couldn't imagine a desert he loved more than strawberry pie. He couldn't imagine a more perfect life.

~=~=~=~=~=~=~=~

So, with that tweak and twinkle of the stars, Jim and Belinda continue to live their separately ordained lives.

This time without regrets or reservations.

Happily. Ever. After.

Beauty is skin deep
Intelligence lies deeper
Faith lives in the soul

Not So Dumb

You know that old joke where the man asks God why He made woman so beautiful and God says so that man would love her, and then the man asks why God made woman so dumb and God answers so that she would love man? Well that joke kinda describes me and Candi. Candi – Candace – is my big sister. She's beautiful and dumb and loves me unconditionally.

How we got to this place in our lives is all too common. I was twelve and Candi was fourteen when our parents died from an overdose. We thought we had seen all the crap life had to sling, until the system fostered us out. Candi was placed in a home where the wife gladly relinquished her wifely duties to Candi. I was warehoused in a group home where I was just a paycheck and a perk.

That very first night in the group home I knew that getting butt-fucked by some jackleg preacher was not my idea of home, discipline or salvation. I wasn't about to wait to be rescued. I became my own super hero – a force to be reckoned with. I learned how to panhandle and scam and work odd jobs for money. I developed my physical strength to keep the predators at bay, and when that wasn't enough I paid in cash – the only other thing Reverend Shit Dick and his kind valued. Now, at fifteen, I look much older. I have the lean, muscular and well-hung body – I might add – of a man.

It's taken three years, but Candi and I found our way back to each other. We've vowed to go it alone – without benefit of well-meaning and exploitive adults in our lives.

Candi and I live in a two-room apartment in an invisible neighborhood where everybody minds their own business and nobody knows anything when any authority comes around. You might think we could do better if we had help, but that had never been our good fortune. Not even our parents kept a roof over our heads. There were times the four of us slept in doorways and abandoned cars. Candi and I were always hungry. Now we've got a place and food in the fridge. We're doing just fine.

Before our reunion, I remembered my sister as pretty and not too bright. Candi at seventeen is downright movie star beautiful: pouty lips, cute nose, sparkling eyes, full breasts, tiny waist, lush hips, and long legs. She's also a total airhead! She once thought she had a defective bag of M&Ms, claiming "all of them have a 'u' and a 'u' smashed together."

I love my sister. And not just because Candi's skewed vision of the world allows her to put up with my shit without question. True, I cosplay, chase poontang and troll the internet under several guises anytime I want, using a neighbor's unsecured Wi-Fi. To my credit, I do drive Candi to and from work, since she never has been able to master driving. And yeah, I know I'm too young to legally drive, but then both of us are way too young to have been fucked over by the grownups in our lives.

Candi is really a great big sister. Not once has she even suggested that I get a real job or go to school. She's just happy not to have to spread her legs to eat and have a place to stay. And she feels privileged to have me to love and protect her. Truth be told, any man with half her intelligence would fall over himself to love and cherish her. Aside from being a knockout, Candi has the sweetest personality ever. And she wouldn't need a protector if she wasn't waitressing at a club where she dresses like a Nubian sex slave. But that just goes to show you how dumb she is when it comes to reasoning things out.

Right now, I'm living my dream. Candi works, I play. Sometimes I feel guilty about not pulling more weight around the place we share, but I've learned to shake it off. I figure some day when I grow up... Nah, I'm not telling that lie. I'm never growing up. Not if it means being like the asshole adults I know.

I'm smart enough to know someday soon I'm gonna want more things than I can get doing the things I do now. And I'm never ever gonna let Candi sell herself to keep me in style. And the chance of becoming somebody's bitch for ten-to-twenty keeps me on the straight and narrow – pretty much. I've learned how to stay under the radar.

So, I got other plans. I've been studying for my GED online. I haven't told Candi. It's a surprise. I will be the first one in our family to make it that far in school. Once I get that GED, I'll have options.

Anyway, that's the future. Right now, it's just after one, on a Sunday morning, and I'm on my way out to the west boonies to The Hole. That's where Candi works.

When I get there, I head in through the service door, bumping knuckles with Omar. Omar is a menacing six-foot-six hulk of a guy.

He only needs to hover over an unruly customer to put him in check. He and his cousin Moses look out for the girls that work here.

"How's it hanging, Hero?" he greets me, using Candi's pet name for me.

"No worries," I say.

"Same here," Omar replies.

On my way to the main club area, I stop to open the peek door to the private room. I'm always rewarded with an ample view of tits and clits here. Tonight, I'm disappointed to see the face attached to one set belongs to Amber. She'd always said the money wasn't good enough to get her to do a private party. I guess the guy who was finger fucking her and creaming her tits had the money to prove her wrong.

I slip into a seat at a rear table in the bar where I can observe the action – not so much what's happening on stage, but what's happening on the club floor. I see Candi shrug off the unwelcome hand feeling her up as she deposits drinks on the table. Moses, a slightly larger version of Omar, steps in to discourage a repeat performance.

Scanning the room, I see Professor Pervert sitting at his usual table, nursing his beer and scribbling and sketching in his leather notebook. This guy showed up the week Candi started working here five months ago. He's been a regular fixture ever since, and according to the cousins, he only sits in Candi's section and always tips her big time.

I watch him. He watches Candi. His eyes rarely leave her as his hands fold the small white square napkin into something. He always gives it to Candi, who oohs and ahhs at his skill. Candi now has dozens of flowers and animals in an old brocade hat box she bought at a yard sale. Each new addition graces her dresser until its replacement comes. Then the old object joins its predecessors in the hat box.

I can't say I like or dislike this guy. I don't know him. And he's made no effort to talk to me, though he knows I'm Candi's brother. Which makes him a pervert in my book. Why's he avoiding me? At first, I thought he was from child protection. That just doesn't seem to fit though. Unless he's cooking up some plan to trade sex from Candi for our freedom. Whatever he's hiding, I'll find out. Whatever scheme he's plotting ain't happening. Candi and I have earned the right to be where we are. An army of Professor Perverts isn't gonna stop us.

~=~=~=~=~=~=~=~

"What's with the freaky napkin birds?" I had asked Candi on the drive home one morning.

"Origami," Candi corrected. "Warren says he likes making beautiful things for me."

"Sounds pretty lame to me. And what's with the notebook? You should watch yourself around him, Candi. He's got this whole shy professor vibe going, and it's probably covering up a latent homosexual serial killer."

Candi giggled. "Where do you get these ideas, Hero? Warren's not a murderer and he's not gay." She offered no qualifying proof. I didn't like her trusting him.

"I don't like it, Candi. Why hasn't he ever said anything to me?"

"Because you're not supposed to be there; you're underage."

"And so are you," I struck back.

"Just by a few months. And no one knows that. My ID says I'm 22," she reminded me. "Hero, you don't have to protect me from Warren. He respects me. He's very smart and he doesn't make me feel dumb. He writes beautiful words about me in his journal. He reads them to me sometimes – on the nights when it's slow. He's a good guy, Hero. Have a little faith in my judgement. I'll let you know if I'm in over my head."

I looked at my sister. Sometimes she sounded so reasonable. But I know she's just too dumb to recognize this pervert's slick shit. I let it go for the moment, and continued to keep a vigilant eye on them at the club.

~=~=~=~=~=~=~=~=~

Professor Pervert kept making napkin birds and flowers for Candi, and giving her big tips. He paid little attention to the strippers on stage and never went to the private room. He lavished all his attention on Candi. It didn't set right with me; I couldn't shake the feeling he was stalking her. That's when I decided to stalk him.

It wasn't easy at first. I couldn't follow him from the club, as he always left just at closing, which meant I had Candi with me. So, I did the next best thing. I went on a fact-finding mission. I got his license plate number from his car. I causally pumped information from others around the club. I listened carefully whenever Candi talked about him. I searched public records online. Within two weeks, I had a profile of Professor Pervert and could start my new daytime pastime – finding out who this man was and why he was stalking my sister.

As it turned out, Warren Jefferson Smith is twenty-seven years old, unmarried and an assistant professor at the community college. He teaches philosophy. He lives alone in a three-bedroom bungalow in a working-class neighborhood. He occasionally bowls with friends from work. Sometimes he goes to campus events or a play or concert. No criminal record I could find, but it's easy to cover up shit with enough money and the right connections. He seems normal – whatever the hell that means. Other than stalking my sister, he doesn't have any red flag extracurricular activities.

I do notice women are seriously attracted to him – students, housewives, clerks in stores, young girls, old women. The pussy is there for the taking. I wouldn't mind being in those shoes. If I were him, I'd have a different bitch every night. But he's not fucking anyone. He just sits and watches Candi. Candi says he's never suggested they use the private room. Maybe he suffers from some weird kind of erectile disease and gets off some other kinky way.

Whatever. After watching Professor Pervert almost three months, I'm still waiting to discover some dirt that I can use to leverage him out of Candi's high opinion of him.

~≍~≍~≍~≍~≍~≍~≍~

Tonight, I swing by the club early. It's midnight when I make my way to the service entrance. I greet Omar as usual, and start down the hallway.

And then it dawns on me what Omar has just said, "I can do without the trouble tonight, Hero."

When I reach the private room, I skip the peek and throw open the door. Candi is sitting on the edge of the couch; Professor Pervert is kneeling between her legs. His arms are wrapped tightly round her waist, and she is stroking his hair, his face is buried in her near naked bosom.

I reach them in one long stride. My hand is in his collar, yanking him off Candi.

"Get off my sister you pervert," I rage, kicking him while he's still down.

Candi is shrieking, "stop, Hero," and rushing to the pervert's aid.

"You don't have to do this for money," I yell at her. "I can get a job."

Before I can get in another lick, Omar is at the door. "Enough, Hero," he booms. "You know who's gonna win this one. I don't wanna hurt you."

"It's alright," the pervert says, the pain in his ribs restricting his speech some. He pulls himself up to a respectable six-foot-two, and guides a shaking Candi back to the couch. He turns to me and points to the velvet hassock. "Sit," he barks.

"We're fine," he tells Omar.

Omar nods. "I'm just outside," he says, closing the door.

I move to get up with the intention of continuing the beat down I had started when Professor Pervert's right fist clips me, knocking me back down on the hassock. "Sit," he tells me again. "Today is Candi's eighteenth birthday. She is legally able to determine the course of her life. Don't ruin it."

I feel like shit. I'd forgotten it was Candi's birthday.

He reaches over to the side table to retrieve a colorful bouquet of origami flowers. He hands them to Candi and kneels before her.

"Of all the women I have known, there has never been one I wanted to bear my children. Candi, you have the grit of a survivor, the soul of an optimist, the conscience of a child and a heart full of forgiveness. All enshrined in a body that would shame a Botticelli. There may be women prettier or smarter than you, but there is no woman better than you. And there is no one better suited for me."

I sat there dumbstruck. The pervert was proposing to my sister!

Then he presents a sparkling diamond ring to Candi. "Please marry me, Candi."

Candi hesitates, looking over his shoulder at me.

"He's your family, and welcome in our home as long as you want," he tells her.

Candi holds out her hand and lets Warren slip the ring on her finger. His arms are around her waist again, holding her tightly to him. This is where I'd barged in, and where I quietly exit.

~=~=~=~=~=~=~=~

Another three years have passed.

Warren took those wedding vows seriously. When he said, "with all my worldly goods I thee endow," he meant it. He gave Candi the deed to his house as a wedding present. I figured he was so pussy whipped that I could carry on as I had been. But the privilege of a home came with rules, which – to my surprise – Candi laid down and enforced with an iron will.

It wasn't easy for me. While Warren and I rarely butted heads, Candi constantly took me to task. I eventually settled down, found my zone and started behaving like a human being – only because I didn't want to lose my sister.

I learned to respect myself in the process. I became someone other people respected and wanted to be around. People who cared and felt beyond the superficial became a mainstay in my life. I got my GED, a part time job, and enrolled in an English class at the college where Warren teaches. Along the way, I discovered what it was to be an adult, a real man. I finally had a good example. I have a girlfriend now – not just some chick I'm banging.

And Candi. Turns out she's not so dumb after all. Shortly after she got pregnant with my nephew Alex, named Alexander after me, Candi had a complete physical including an eye examine. Turns out she has a condition called monocular vision dysfunction, which causes her to see double images. No wonder she had trouble reading and driving! Long story short, now she wears glasses with corrective prisms and reads at least two books a week. And she drives.

And Warren. He was the first adult who changed our lives in a positive way. He saw past Candi's beauty and my terrible teens. He's no fool either. He had known that I was tailing him those months before he proposed. He's never called me out on it in front of Candi, though. After he and Candi got engaged, Warren made it clear to me that he might be a Boy Scout in some respects, but he wasn't born yesterday. If I caused Candi one sleepless night, I would answer to him.

But with all the education and rhetoric at his disposal, Warren couldn't explain how he ended up at The Hole. When he came in that first time, he thought it would be a one-off adventure. Then he saw Candi and he was hooked. It's doubtful Warren would have met either of us anywhere else. There was no other common ground.

Again, I remember my first night in the group home, sitting with my knees drawn up, back to the brick wall, scared to go to sleep, listening to the desperate cries around me. I remember praying for a home, someplace safe for me and Candi. Someplace where we could just be normal.

And it dawns on me – all this has been all about that ask. And Warren is the godsend.

Spare me your disdain
Check your hatred at the door
Let me live my life

Tick-Tock

Unlike the day before, John Fremont lingered on the park bench, invisibly rooted to the spot, unwilling to finish the brown-bagged lunch and return to the office. Today, as he had done often in the past month, John took stock of his life and did not like the results: he looked older than his thirty-four years, and each morning he felt anxious and tired from the moment he opened his eyes. The wife he no longer adored, but still loved, was pregnant with their third and fourth child – two more boys – enough for a polo team if circumstance and finance had favored him.

The prestigious title of "Branch Manager, Mariners Bank and Trust", conveyed none of the pressures of the job. The fear of making a mistake that would unbalance every account overshadowed the magic in modeling with pivot tables. To say John was dissatisfied with his life and lot was an understatement.

Across town, just like every day for the past eight years, Alice Fremont found herself standing in Marvin's Produce Market, sniffing, squeezing and pinching the fruits and vegetables. And just like every day for the past six years she was not alone: having either a child in utero, in tow or both. It was difficult for Alice to remember a time when she was alone – with only her thoughts and desires paramount. She loved her husband and children, but she felt that with each day she was losing herself. She no longer recognized the reflection in the mirror: a lifeless woman filled with life – two more sons to join Team Testosterone. She wondered if she would feel so lost if she were carrying daughters.

Today was Wednesday, so she would prepare a salad of micro greens, melon and avocado, dressed with a handcrafted herb vinaigrette. Her husband, whom she loved with all her heart, but was no longer in love with, would prepare some meat or fish on the grill. Everything perfectly prescribed and executed – like clockwork. To say she was forlorn did not do justice to the overwhelming feeling of despair enveloping her.

That evening, dinner dishes done, and their boys sleeping peacefully in the upstairs bedroom, John and Alice sat silently in their back yard. Each thought about the deck they had discussed earlier in the week: John knew it would necessitate uprooting the massive oak with its comforting shade; Alice knew it would make their home as indistinct as the surrounding houses. Still, they each reasoned, it was a small concession to make for solidarity. *Wasn't it?* Each said nothing, and after sitting together for hours, lonely for the John and Alice they had once been, retired to another night of unrestful slumber.

~=~=~=~=~=~

Emon Zein had been in America just two short years. He had come to live in this small Midwestern town by chance – his car had broken down several miles from the outskirts. This chance circumstance had proved to be fortuitous. He had established himself as a skilled artisan, settling into a modest clock shop with lodgings above, in the lower downtown district. His days were spent in his shop. His customers were few, but enough to sustain his needs. His evenings were spent exploring – accepting the hospitality of new acquaintances and learning about this new homeland. He had so much to learn and assimilate: speech patterns and idioms, clothing styles, popular culture. These were mere trifles. Emon had known extreme poverty and oppressive policies. Here, in America, the Promise abounded and he took solace in that.

Tonight, though the hour was late, after Emon left the company of the church family that had befriended him, he indulged himself with a stroll through the neighborhood of well-kept homes at the northernmost section of the town. To say Emon was content barely scratched the surface of his joy.

~=~=~=~=~=~

Alice woke, as she usually did just after midnight, with the urge to empty her bladder – yet another sign that her body was not her own to control. Her nightgown, damp with sweat from the stifling heat and humidity, clung to her disproportioned body as she shuffled across the bedroom to the master bath.

When she finished relieving herself, instead of returning to bed, Alice went downstairs to the kitchen for a glass of juice. She paused at the patio doors. The not quite dead embers of the grilling pit caught her eye. Alice walked out to the yard and over to the fire pit where she took its poker. Continuing to the grill she thought about how desperately she wanted someone to care about her without asking about the children. Alice began stirring the coals in the grill, lost in thoughts that shamed her, not realizing a few of the fiery embers had landed at the foot of her gown. It wasn't until the fabric had ignited that Alice recognized her peril. Frantically she screamed and flailed about, giving life to the flames.

From the bedroom window, John saw the man, dark as night, leap over the hedge, at once ripping the gown from Alice and smothering the flames. Alice fell to the ground at Emon's feet trembling and screaming.

Alice's screams carried through the warm night air, bringing neighbors in various stages of undress to her aid. The yard soon was bathed in flood lights turned on by the frantic motion of a dozen people. Emon was dragged away from Alice and thrown to the ground, the muzzle of a hunting rifle pressed to his forehead. Someone covered Alice with a blanket and led her to the chaise.

"He raped her," someone shouted.

"That jigaboo was going to burn her alive. Look at her nightgown."

"Kill the coon."

"No! Burn him!"

The voices grew louder and more malevolent.

"No, no," Emon cried, "I did not..." Before he could finish, the butt of a rifle slammed into the side of his face.

"You damn right jigga, we stopped you before you could."

Emon shook his head. *What was this madness?* He watched as a garden hose was fashioned into a noose and thrown over the ancient oak. Another person scanned the area with a cell phone – proudly taping this grotesque injustice.

All the while this scene unfolded, Alice sat huddled on the chaise, her next-door neighbor protectively shielding her and stroking her hair. Alice felt alive. SHE was the star – the focus of attention.

John rushed from the house to a cacophony of voices relating a tale he knew to be absolute fiction. Emon was pulled to his knees and the rifle shoved into John's hands.

"Kill that Africoon," they vehemently urged John.

"Don't let Jim Fish get away with it."

"It's your right," someone reasoned.

"We can't let his kind ruin the things we cherish," another voice cried out.

"If you let him go, his kind will rape and kill us all in our sleep one day."

"We must protect ourselves. No one else will."

John felt powerfully alive. HE was in control. Alice, assisted by a neighbor came to stand beside her husband. John pointed the rifle at the ground in front of the innocent man who had saved his wife and unborn sons. John eased the bullet into the chamber and moved his finger to the trigger.

Emon no longer struggled. He considered each fearful black face in that yard and wondered if prosperity had crafted the inhumanity he saw. When he had first come upon this tiny hamlet of East Gate, he had imagined he had found Mecca. It became his vision: someday he would own one of these homes, with its professionally manicured lawn. He would have a beautiful wife, and children to carry on his legacy. Now he saw these Black Americans and their lifestyle as a perversion, an irony. He was not to be given a chance; his fate had been decided because he did not belong to their world. *So be it!* If this was to be his last stand, it would be without illusions.

Emon's gaze rested on the woman he had saved from the fire and the man beside her with the rifle. He knew the woman knew the truth. He saw in the man's eyes that he, too, knew Emon's true deed. *Why do they not speak for me?* His heart sank. His red-rimmed eyes challenged the absurdity of the situation.

"My honor lives," Emon spoke to the wind. He closed his eyes; he would not beg for that to which he was entitled. That was his pride.

~~~~~~~~~~~~

Seven years to the day, John looked at his pocket watch as he emerged from the Midwest Savings and Loan. He smiled and greeted passersby before heading to Timepieces in the next block. As he reached the door, Emon Zein emerged, carrying two gaily wrapped packages.

"To celebrate the seventh birthday of my godsons," he said to John, handing him the gifts as he locked the door of his shop.

John nodded his appreciation of the gifts. "They will love whatever it is because it comes from you," he told his friend.

The men proceeded to Emon's car, parked in the lot across the street. They drove in a comfortable silence, arriving twenty minutes later in Emon's driveway. Emon's wife Dalila was watering the baobabs that stood sentry on the porch, while Alice sat watching her boys play soccer.

Seeing the presents tucked under Emon's arm, the younger boys immediately abandoned the game to run to him.

"Peetpa! Peetpa, what did you bring us?" the twins said in unison. They had reached Emon, wrapping their arms around their godfather. Emon gave each of them a present and joyfully watched them drop where they stood and excitingly unwrap them.

"Thank you, Peetpa," said Joshua.

"Thank you, Peetpa," echoed Gabriel.

The two men joined their wives on the porch, exchanging hugs and hellos.

That such a friendship had forged between the two men was remarkable. That night, seven years ago, as John was about to allow an unspeakable injustice, his twin boys cried out from Alice's womb to champion their savior. Alice's water broke, and her labor diverted the attention from Emon to her.

John had dropped the rifle and caught his wife as her knees buckled from the sudden pain. He carried her to the chaise, laying her down gently.

"Let him go!" John shouted, as he saw two neighbors grab hold of Emon. "I saw it all from the upstairs window. This man saved Alice and the babies. Her nightgown caught fire from the charcoals. Forgive me," he implored of Emon, "I should have spoken up sooner."

Emon was released, but there were no other apologies from the frenzied neighbors. Just fault levied at Emon, because he was not one of their own:

> "I've never seen him in the neighborhood before. How was I to know he wasn't a rapist and murderer?"

> "Well, he could have said something before things escalated."

> "His accent is to blame. Who could understand what he was saying?"

Those inexcusable excuses for their vigilante behavior soothed what conscious they had.

And then, for a second time that night, Emon saved Alice and the babies.

As Alice lay on the chaise, her knees drawn up and parted, Emon noticed the small hand and arm protruding from the birth canal. In his thickly accented and broken English Emon spoke, then gestured the urgency of the situation.

John looked into the eyes of this stranger, who could have turned his back and walked away, but chose to stay. "Do it," John nodded his consent. Changing positions, he knelt beside the chaise, a supporting arm around Alice's shoulders, his free hand holding hers.

Sitting on the chaise at her feet, Emon's fingers nimbly inched into Alice's vagina until nothing of his hand and wrist was visible. Remembering how he had turned goats in utero, amid Alice's tortured screams, Emon applied the same technique and successfully turned the baby to its proper birthing position. Joshua was delivered before the ambulance arrived. Gabriel made his entrance into the world at the hospital.

After that night, the residents of East Gate let their collective, unacknowledged guilt lead them to patronize the small clock shop, further building Emon's reputation as a skilled horologist. Emon repaired and restored clocks and watches from the wealthiest East Gate families. With the help of his new friend John, Emon expanded his shop with an Internet storefront, and began building custom timepieces for a global clientele.

Emon prospered. He had a house, not in East Gate, but in a neighborhood where the feeling of family and belonging prevailed. He had a wife, and they were expecting their first child. The Promise was fulfilling.

John and Alice prospered as well. It took getting lost for them to find their way. They no longer lived in East Gate; they bought the house across the street from the Zeins five years ago. Their boys – all four – were happy and healthy. John loved his job, and Alice took great satisfaction from her roles at home and in the community.

Time would tell how happily ever after they all would be.

Careful who you hurt
Payback makes victors losers
Your win is now hers

Game On

Marty couldn't shake the feeling that he knew the gorgeous woman seated at the window booth at Emma's Kitchen. His eyes were immediately drawn to her lovely pouty lips – lips painted a warm color that reminded him of maple syrup. He imagined they would taste just as good.

She looked up, just as he was fantasizing about kissing those lips, and smiled.

No further encouragement was needed. Marty left his corner table, bringing his half-filled mug of coffee, and scooted into the seat opposite her.

"I know we've met before...and I'm a fool for not remembering where," he said.

"No," she replied. There was a hint of a southern drawl which made 'no' sound like a multi-syllabic word.

"I'm sure of it," Marty insisted. "Was it at the Du for the Kwanzaa celebration?"

"No," she said again.

While Marty was perfectly content to watch those lips continue to say 'no', he was just as eager to coax out a 'yes'.

"How about we start over. I'm sure it'll come to me eventually." Marty extended his hand across the table, "I'm Martin Washington. Marty."

"Desiree DePriest," she said, her hand meeting his.

The way she spoke her name was musical. Marty was beginning to believe that they hadn't met before. There was no way he could have forgotten her.

"Desiree," he repeated, enjoying the sound of her name. "I may be wrong. But there's something about you that seems so familiar."

"I've had a few roles in local theater productions," she offered. "Right now, I have a second understudy role in the ensemble cast of Hamilton."

"No way! I just saw that a week ago – Saturday evening performance on the fourteenth. Were you on that night?"

"No, I've yet to perform," Desiree said wistfully, her accent tickling her words provocatively.

The waitress came over to the table with a pot of coffee to top off Marty's mug and another glass of sweet tea for Desiree. "Can I get you anything else?" she asked, ready to leave the checks on the table.

Marty shot a questioning glance at Desiree. "Something sweet maybe? It's on me."

Desiree looked across the café at the covered cake dishes lined along the back counter. "I'd like the limoncello cake," she told the waitress, then turned to Marty and added, "but only if you'll share it with me."

"A slice of limoncello cake and two forks," he confirmed the order with the waitress.

~~~~~~~~~~~~

A half-hour later, the cake eaten and their checks paid – Marty gallantly paid both, including a generous tip – the two chatted amicably as they strolled down the street towards the lakefront.

About five blocks into their walk, Desiree stopped in front of a three-story French chateau townhouse. "I live here," she gestured to the building, "third floor."

Marty was contemplating his next move when Desiree suggested, "Would you like to come upstairs and rehydrate? How does a bottle of Hildon sound?"

"Sounds like just what I need to quench my thirst," he said.

As Marty climbed the stairs behind Desiree he couldn't shake the feeling of déjà vu. Inside the apartment, Desiree left him in the living room, excusing herself to go to the kitchen. She returned with two bottles of Hildon, two glasses and a small bowl of ice. Desiree placed the tray containing these items on the sofa table.

"I acquired a taste for Hildon when I was studying theater in Manchester."

Desiree added several ice cubes to a glass and poured water over them. She handed the glass to Marty.

Marty took the glass and looked at Desiree, puzzled.

"Didn't you want ice?" she asked. "You drank your water with ice at the café."

"No. It's fine," he said, accepting the glass. He watched her pour the remainder of the bottle into the second glass and move over to the French doors which opened out onto a balcony. "You're very observant," he commented.

"Most actors are. We tend to be people watchers." Desiree opened the doors and stepped out onto the balcony.

Marty joined her. "Nice view of the park."

"Yes, it is," she said, then exclaimed, "Oh!" She waved at a woman crossing the street and heading for the building. "That's my oldest sister, Deborah. She's a buyer at Neiman's. She lives in the first-floor apartment. Our middle sister lives on the second floor. She's a research fellow at Northwestern. Fun fact about us: there's a year and nine months difference between her and Deborah's ages; there's the same age difference between my middle sister and me. We all have the exact same birthmark, as well. How's that for a bit of family trivia?"

"Fascinating." *Not a complete lie,* Marty justified to himself. His mind was wandering. He was captivated by the cadence of Desiree's voice and the movement of her mouth as the words pushed past her lips.

Even from a distance, Marty could see the older sister was hot. He wondered about the middle sister. Deborah returned Desiree's wave and entered the building. Marty heard doors open and close below.

He sat his glass on the wrought iron table. "You have the most kissable looking lips," he breathed against her cheek.

Marty's lips brushed Desiree's – gently, almost reverently. The taste was a natural sweetness like honey. He sucked on her lower lip, savoring its warm plump flesh, then he slowly penetrated her yielding mouth with his tongue. Their tongues danced a slow tentative prelude before plunging into a quickened tempo that hovered between passion and desire.

Desiree.

When their lips parted, he watched the freckled tip of her tongue seductively caress her upper lip.

And then he remembered. Denise. Denise Something-or-Other. Black-rimmed Coke-bottle-thick glasses, painfully shy. A girl geek. And freckles on the tip of her tongue. He remembered that tongue doing some amazingly wicked things in his mouth and on his dick. *Damn, she's changed! But that tongued certainly hasn't — I'd know it anywhere.*

And then Marty remembered more. Four years back. He had been an absolute ass with Denise. He had been drinking and hooked up with her on a dare and a bet. And then ducked her phone calls. And then pretended to not know who she was when he saw her in the same bar a few weeks later. *Had she been rocking this banging body under those baggy clothes back then?* Gosh he wished he could remember more of that first encounter.

"Denise," he began, "I..."

"Desiree," she corrected.

No. That couldn't be. What were the odds that two women would have the same unique freckling? And could kiss like that?

"Look," he began, putting some distance between them, "I admit that I didn't remember you at first. You look so different," he stammered, his hand sweeping in a head-to-toe gesture. "Look, you don't have to play this game. I admit I was an asshole. I would never want a guy treating my sister the way I treated you. I apologize."

Marty grabbed his glass of water from the table and took a long swallow. Fortified, he looked Desiree in the eye and said, "I'm not the same guy I was back then. I was immature, drunk and stupid to boot. That's not an excuse for the way I behaved. I'm just saying that younger me was full of himself and thoughtless. I apologize," he said for the second time.

"Then apologize to Denise," Desiree replied. She stepped back into the apartment.

Marty was right behind her. He followed Desiree's gaze to the alcove by the front door. The woman standing there looked like Desiree. Marty's eyes went back and forth between the two women. Same height and coloring. Where Desiree had those voluptuous curves, this one was more athletic in build – still, very attractive.

He finished the glass of water, sucking on the remnant of a nearly dissolved piece of ice. He set the glass on the tray and moved closer to the other woman. It was Denise. But what an upgrade! Gone were the oversized geeky glasses and desperate and diminutive body language. This woman was beautiful, poised and exuding confidence. Denise 2.0 was dope!

"The middle sister," he said aloud, but more to himself. He suddenly realized the web he had stepped into.

"Hello, Martin."

He winced at the sound of his given name. He felt like he was being chastised. "Denise," he said, moving in to kiss her cheek.

Denise side-stepped him to stand next to her sister. "Really?" she asked incredulously.

"Okay, you got me. I was a jerk and a fool. I hurt and humiliated you for no good reason. Please believe that I regret my behavior. Please accept my apology."

"Apology accepted. Now goodbye, Martin."

"Goodbye, Marty," Desiree said.

"That's it?" Marty asked.

"An apology is all I need," Denise said, her lips curved in a satisfying smile.

"What did you expect, Marty?" Desiree's drawl teased.

"That all would be forgiven and forgotten, Martin? That we would just pick up where we left off?" Denise scoffed.

"Or did you think that you and I might heat up the sheets, Marty?" Desiree asked.

"You couldn't possibly think that the three of us..."

"Ewww! No way that ever could happen!" Desiree interrupted, nipping that fantasy in the bud.

Marty's pulse quickened and his head ached as he followed the conversation from one sister to the other. The thought of a sensuous sister sandwich whetted his appetite. Perhaps he could have the oldest sister on the side. The thought was dizzying. Perspiration sprouted on his forehead. He felt oddly intoxicated. But he'd only had water. Over ice.

The ice!

Desiree opened the front door and Denise gently shoved Marty across the threshold. Marty grabbed the bannister for support. He stumbled down the stairs, Denise and Desiree followed him. It seemed like forever had come and gone when he finally reached the first-floor landing. The door was open. Deborah stood there, her arms folded under her ample breasts. She gave him a disapproving sneer and childishly stuck out her tongue at him.

Freckles!

Marty grabbed at the moving blur of the doorknob on the entry door. After several tries he managed to open it and escape to the outside. His lungs gulped air as he grasped the iron railing to support his descent to the sidewalk.

He turned to look back at the building. The three sisters stood on the stoop, arms around each other's waist. One by one, each blew him a kiss, wiggled her fingers and said "bye-bye" before exiting stage rear into the townhouse.

Marty steadied his aching head between his palms. *Lesson learned* he told himself. He was lucky to have dodged a more lethal bullet. He shivered at the thought of waking up in an alley with his severed penis in his pocket. That would have been much worse than the drug induced headache he was nursing.

Yeah, lesson learned. Maybe he still had a chance with one of the sisters. After all, his apology was accepted, and those freckled tongues were a major draw. *Next time I'll play my hand differently,* Marty counseled himself as he judiciously made his way up the street.

Remember your roots
They make sense of the senseless
And quell true evil

Welcome Home, Son

Ruana Meeks regretted many things. There was the time when she had not stopped that fool Bé-Bé Charles from taunting that little white girl on the bus. Had she interfered, perhaps the child would be alive and Bé-Bé wouldn't be sitting on death row.

It seemed that whenever Ruana knew she should risk using her gifts and didn't, the consequences were catastrophic. The years and regrets should have drilled that lesson home.

Still, Ruana hadn't heeded the signs.

Ruana operated under the misguided belief that the old ways and her gifts were an anachronism. Modern society had no place for divination and spelling. Law and justice served society.

She now knew better.

They had gone swiftly to trial, but there was barely a day of evidence and testimony before the "not guilty" verdict. How could the drug and alcohol fueled hit and run slaughter of her son be dismissed so capriciously? What brand of justice was this?

Ruana had listened to the defense lawyer twist everything to favor his privileged client. "Why," Lawyer Talbot questioned, "was

Clifton Meeks dressed all in black, walking an unfamiliar road in the dead of night?" The implication that her son purposely tried to conceal his presence in the upscale neighborhood was not lost on the jurors. Ruana sensed them reason that her son's murderer had performed a public service by stopping a potential threat.

The prosecution's objections and explanations fell on deaf ears. The jurors weren't interested to know that Clifton's attire was the uniform all the hired servers had worn that evening, that Clifton had stayed behind to finish cleaning around the pool and missed his ride. The jurors were too invested in the "poor little rich boy" drama manipulatively woven by the defense.

Clifton had no champions. The people he had worked for that evening conveniently were out of town during the trail, offering only a dispassionate written account of his presence that night. The lines were drawn, and Clifton Meeks was not in the inner circle.

As the final remarks by prosecution and defense were spoken, Ruana saw the sympathy in the eyes of the jurors – not for her or her son, dead before his time – but for that piece of worthless humanity who, according to Lawyer Talbot, "would bear the trauma of the unfortunate accident for the rest of his life."

So, the verdict was no surprise. Ruana left the courtroom amid the triumphant smiles and congratulations across the aisle.

She left to go home and prepare.

~=~=~=~=~=~=~=~

DAILY NEWS | 04/15/2017 03:12 CDT

Dale Hargrove, 22, acquitted just last week in the vehicular homicide of 18-year-old Clifton Meeks remains in a coma after hitting a tree in rural Rockford County. Hargrove was airlifted to University Hospital. Doctors there are not optimistic about his recovery.

DAILY NEWS | 04/19/2017 21:14 CDT

Mystery surrounds the death of Dale Hargrove, 22, heir to the Hargrove hotel dynasty. The family attorney would only confirm that life support was removed at two o'clock Sunday afternoon.

A source close to the family revealed that the brain-dead Hargrove was inexplicably drained of three-fourths of his blood volume, and an MRI scan showed that his heart was missing. "What was there was dark and shriveled. It resembled a lump of coal," the anonymous source said.

Doctors and police have "no comment."

~=~=~=~=~=~=~=~

Ruana Meeks stopped hanging the bedsheets on the line and looked down the road. She saw the figure – tall, male – slowly make his way to her. By the time he reached her, she had finished hanging the rest of the laundry.

He was gaunt and smelled of modern science – nothing her cooking and herbal cleanses couldn't cure. His eyes took everything in. These new surroundings sparked questions too numerous to answer at once.

"Welcome home, Son." Ruana smiled and embraced Clifton. She led him towards the house. "Let me tell you about the last few weeks."

Once in a lifetime
Existing before they knew
Their love is timeless

Bro Code

Philip, Marcus, Edgar and I have been friends since kindergarten at St. Jerome's. We have survived war, marriage, births, deaths, divorce, illness, unemployment, career changes, mid-life angsts and bad investments. We are card-carrying members of an association without a name other than friendship. Our bro code, the only rules we have ever held sacred are 1) if any of us is ever in jail, the others will bail him out – unless the offense is murdering a relative; and 2) our sisters are off limits – unless marriage is the end game.

So, when we four met up at Comache's Barbershop for our equivalent of a spa day: shave, haircut and manicure, our conversation touched on all the things men of our generation deem important. Some things never change. We joked and laughed and generally behaved as we had in our twenties.

The conversation drifted to Marcus' quandary over his daughter's mystery guy.

"She's seeing some loser she's too ashamed to bring by the house for us to meet," he lamented.

"Maybe not." I offered a different perspective. "Could be they're not serious. You know kids these days. Sex without commitment is de rigueur. Come to think of it, that's not much different from the way we were. You remember. Sex, drugs and rock 'n' roll."

"And what makes you think my baby is doing drugs and having sex with this degenerate?" he roared at me.

I held up my hands in surrender. When Marcus goes into protective overdrive, it's best not to fan the flames.

"Marcus, you can't assume that just because Nicole doesn't want you scaring the piss out of her young man that he's a deadbeat," Edgar added, trying to take the conversation down a notch. Edgar and his first ex-wife are Nicole's godparents.

"I'm seeing Nicole," Phil announced.

Everything stopped. Scissors, clippers, razors and emery boards halted in midmotion. You could have heard a mouse pissing on cotton, it was so quiet. Everyone looked at me, then Marcus.

Let me explain. Nicole is my niece; Marcus is married to my sister, Rhonda, and Nicole is their twenty-six-year-old daughter.

"Not funny, Phil," I warned.

"I'm not joking," he replied.

Marcus still hadn't said anything. He sat upright from the reclined chair, shaving cream still on his face. The guy shaving him exchanged a worried look with the gal buffing Phil's nails.

I imagine everyone was thinking the same thing. *Are you fucking crazy!?* Thoughts of my lifelong friend having sex with a hot young girl less than half his age would have garnered high-fives all around. But this was my niece. She was as off-limits as her mother had been.

My brother-in-law eased off the chair and stood over Phil. Phil rose to look him square in the eye. Everyone eased back to give them room. In college, Marcus had been an impressive cruiserweight boxer. He and Phil still sparred at the local gym. That camaraderie was totally absent now.

"I love her." Phil said.

Phil was always a man of few words. He pulled a ring box out of his pants pocket and flipped it open. Jaws dropped at the five carat IIa diamond in its antique platinum setting.

"I'm asking her tonight," Phil continued. "You guys know the man I am. Nicole is a grown woman. It's her choice."

Phil closed the ring box, put it back in his pocket and sat down. Marcus was still standing, clenching and unclenching his fist.

The four of us have known each other longer than Nicole has been in this world. Phil has never chased women the way the rest of us have. He's always been the bachelor of the group, and we have convinced our girlfriends and wives over the years to just let him be. None of the matchmaking ever worked. He always seemed to be waiting for that special someone.

Now, after all this time, Phil was in love. His someone special was Nicole. He was willing to risk it all for her. Because whether Nicole said 'yes' or 'no', things might never be the same with us four. God knows I love my wife, but I have never loved a woman that much, and I don't know if I ever could. All I could think of was if Marcus remembered how things were when he knew Rhonda was the one, then surely, he would cut Phil some slack.

Marcus turned his back to Phil, dropped his head and squared his shoulders. When he turned to face his friend, he moved over to the swivel stool the manicurist had vacated and sat down.

"You're a good man, Phil," Marcus said, holding out his hand. "If my daughter turns you down, she's a fool."

The collective sigh of relief could probably be heard next door. Our conversation picked up as if the defining moment we had just stared down had never threatened our friendship. We slipped into a familiar pattern of giving advice on how to pull off a romantic proposal – something we'd always done for one another. Three times so far for Edgar.

~=~=~=~=~=~=~=~

Nicole said "yes", of course, and she and Phil were married six months later. They had two boys and a girl over the next four years. Then Phil had a vasectomy saying his family was complete, and it was an easier procedure for him than anything Nicole would have to undergo. Besides, he wanted Nicole to be able to have more children if she wanted, if something should happen to him.

Nicole and Phil saw their first two grandchildren, two beautiful girls, courtesy of their older son. As fate would have it, a freak accident on IL-41 took Nicole shortly before her sixty-fifth birthday. They had been married thirty-eight years. Phil died of a broken heart a week later at the age of ninety-one. It was the longest they had ever been apart.

Of the four of us, only Edgar and I are left. We still live by our code: if one of us gets arrested, the other will bail him out – unless the offense is murdering a relative; and our sisters are off limits – unless marriage is the end game.

I remind Edgar of this second rule often, as Rhonda is a widow, and Edgar is single yet again.

Crazy is as crazy does
No time for your shit
Dealing with my own

Lies That Bind

The first lie I ever told was to protect my Mama. I was five. I had walked home from kindergarten on my own.

I had waited for Mama that day, impatiently watching everyone else head home with their parent or older sibling. I knew my way home, so I just decided to go it alone. Well, not all alone. I trailed behind the Johnsons who lived on my block. There were nine of them, but only six were in the elementary school I attended – the other three were in high school.

I remember, every few steps, Barbara Ann, who was in my class, would glance over her shoulder to see if I was still there. When the Johnson clan turned into their front yard I walked the half block down to my house, a bundle of excitement and dread – very proud of my successful adventure, yet a little afraid of what I might find.

As I approached my house, I saw my Daddy rush desperately out the front door. He smiled when he saw me. He didn't say anything, just took my hand and walked with me into the house.

Mama was in the kitchen, manically moving between table and stove, chopping vegetables and stirring pots. I remember Mama being upset that I hadn't waited for her, and Daddy being upset that Mama had forgotten to pick me up. They yelled at each. Daddy said he had enough and was leaving. And he was taking me with him.

Mama said that I would never leave her, that I loved her more. She turned to me for confirmation.

My Daddy calmly asked, "You'll come with Daddy, won't you?"

And that was when I lied. "No, Daddy. I can't leave Mama. I'm staying with her."

I saw the hurt in my Daddy's eyes, and he saw the tears forming in mine. I knew that he knew I was lying to protect Mama's feelings. Mama gloated, and I wished I had been brave enough to tell her the truth: that I loved my Daddy much more, I could depend on him, and I would follow him to the ends of the earth. But I knew she needed me more.

Daddy understood. He didn't leave for another seven years. *Bless you, Daddy, for sticking it out for as long as you did.*

~≍~≍~≍~≍~≍~≍~≍~

I got used to Mama's mood swings – her bouts of depression and euphoria. I remember one incident vividly. I was in junior high, and had been at band practice after school, rehearsing for our winter concert. My throat was sore, I had a bit of a chill, I was exhausted, and in no mood for Mama's drama when I got home.

Mama had spent the day making chicken soup from scratch – just for me – and had set an elaborate table to showcase her love and devotion. I told her I wasn't hungry and just wanted to go to bed. Mama took the bowl of soup from the table and dumped it over my head. "If you don't want to eat it, you can wear it!" she screamed at me.

I didn't say a word to Mama, just left and walked the half-block to Barbara Ann's house. Her parents called Daddy and rushed me to the hospital. I had strep pneumonia.

Mama was very contrite and her version of what happened cast me as the willful, unmanageable pre-teen. She reveled in the sympathy and advice given by the doctors and nurses. Even after they learned the real story, Mama cleverly used her "condition" to justify her behavior and bolster support.

Even so, when I was well enough to leave the hospital, I went home with Mama. She needed me.

~=~=~=~=~=~=~=~

Later in high school, I learned about bipolar disorders, heredity and co-dependency. I promised God and myself that I would try not to lie to spare Mama's feelings or support her delusions.

An opportunity to make good on that vow presented itself one spring day.

Mama and I were walking up the steps to the train platform at Fullerton station. The man in front of us, visibly drunk, was stuffing his wallet in his back pocket. A twenty-dollar bill fell out. I was about to tell the man, but Mama gave me a stern "no" look, and scooped up the bill. "Manna from heaven," she said.

"No," I countered. I took the bill from Mama, tapped the man on the shoulder, told him he had dropped his money and handed it back to him. He gruffly took it from me without so much as a "thank you."

Mama chastised me as we waited for the train. "Are you crazy? We could've had a nice lunch, or gone to the movies. Why are you always doing the opposite of what I tell you? Why do you constantly defy me? Does it make you happy to take away any happiness I find?"

Before I could answer, a man standing within earshot said, "young woman you were right to return that money. I admire your character." He handed me his business card and told me to call him anytime for a reference.

Mama tells the story differently, of course. In her version, the man who dropped the money was verbally abusive to me when I returned the money – at her insistence, of course. The bystander came to our aid, praising Mama's integrity, and offering a reward for her shining example – which she humbly refused, of course.

No matter. That day I consciously began managing our relationship. For my own sake, as much as hers.

~=~=~=~=~=~=~=~

Thirty-six years after that first lie, Mama is still plagued by extreme highs and lows, and an insatiable need to be right at whatever the cost. Medication only works for so long before it becomes ineffective.

What has changed over the years is my willingness to enable Mama's craziness. I just don't have the energy. My plate is already full. I must manage my own brand of crazy.

Do not be afraid
Love's never always perfect
And that is its charm

Love and Larry Freeman

When I declared that Larry Freeman was dead to me, I meant it figuratively. Fate and circumstance schemed differently.

Ours had been a tumultuous rollercoaster ride of a relationship. Lasting all of nine months, it began wildly intoxicating and ended morbidly depressing. What went wrong? Everything. Nothing. It was hard to explain at the time. But it just wasn't working.

"Every man you'll ever know will remind you of me," were his parting words.

And he had been right. Six cities and half a dozen boyfriends later proved the truth of his curse. Each one had ended because he – Larry Freeman – had reared his ugly head and spoiled the relationship.

Not that Larry had been there physically stalking me. No, Larry was skulking around in my mind, which was far worse.

It began with my first post-Larry tryst. I had been dating a mail carrier in my hometown of Chicago. Evan was the nicest of human beings. He cheerfully delivered my mail through Chicago's blustery winter and torrential spring rains. A glass of sweet tea during the sweltering summer heat and a chance meeting at a neighborhood festival placed our casual connection on a totally different plane.

Soon we were enjoying concerts in the park, museum crawls, slasher movies and swims along the lakefront. An autumn weekend in Galena was planned to take our relationship to the next level.

Fall in Galena is a bountiful explosion of colors, tastes, sounds and smells. Autumn breezes and meaty chili and crisp apples and pumpkin spices and fresh-cut timber and crunching leaves all contribute to a sensory overload that can only be calmed by intense physical activity.

After an afternoon of leisurely antiquing, we found ourselves back at our B&B, engaged in what the romance novelists politely define as 'the throes of passion', when out of the blue Evan whispers in my ear, "no one else on my route fucks as good as you."

Even though I had no expectations about our relationship, not even it being monogamous at this point, I didn't like the idea that I was competing in some kind of qualifying game. And, too, this sounded so much like something Larry had once said: "I've fucked a lot of women, but you're the best."

Several things ran through my mind: should I challenge Evan's remark, should I thank him for the compliment, or should I terminate this relationship here and now?

What I did was disengage myself and ask, "What did you say?"

Evan looked puzzled. "I said, 'I can't believe my luck – meeting you on my route, like I did.' Why? What's the matter?"

"Nothing," I lied. I left the bed and walked over to the dresser. Taking a nail file from my toiletry bag, I mulled over my choices as I attacked an imaginary hangnail.

Evan came to stand behind me, enfolding me in his strong arms and warm masculine scent.

"I remind you of him, don't I?"

"Just STOP," I shouted, squirming out of Evan's arms.

"What did I do?" Evan exclaimed, his concern genuine. "I just said that you remind me of everything I love about autumn..."

"It's not you, it's me," I lied again. It wasn't me either. It was Larry!

I didn't wait for a third opportunity to lie. I packed my bag and took the next train back to Chicago – leaving Evan wondering what he had done wrong.

Once home, I frantically gathered everything remotely associated with Larry Freeman and burned it. Still, it did not exorcise him. He continued to haunt me. Coward that I am, I intentionally avoided Evan the next several weeks, then moved to Indianapolis without a forwarding address.

While my job as a senior editor for Kendan Press affords me the freedom of working from anywhere in the world connected to the Internet, I soon tired of the constant state of flux my life had become. Indianapolis and schoolteacher Marco ended in much the same way.

Just as it did with sports writer Gerald in Denver, organic farmer William in Sioux City, bookseller Jesse in Kalamazoo, and artist Julian in Louisville. As soon as things were progressing in a positive, healthy direction, dysfunction reared its ugly head in the form of Larry's taunting.

I had had enough! Larry Freeman had to die. With the decision made, I needed a foolproof plan. It didn't take long to contrive. I simply would lead Larry by his egotistical dick into an inescapable trap and get rid of him once and for all.

It was time to go back to Chicago and face my demon.

~=~=~=~=~=~=~=~

"Took you long enough, but I knew you'd come back." Larry said these words with the casual confidence of a man satisfied that his power over me was everlasting.

To my credit, it only took a three-word text – I need you – to begin the charade that would bring closure to the last thirty-one hellish months. Larry quickly texted back: meet you @ cafe 230.

So here we sat, side by side in 'our booth' tucked back in the corner by the kitchen, drinking lattes. My lips smiled as my mind entertained visions of a dead Larry Freeman.

"We never should've broke up," he continued. "What got into you?"

Fortunately, due to our shoulder to shoulder position, Larry couldn't see the rage in my eyes.

"I don't know," was all I managed to say.

"Well. No matter," he shrugged. "We're back together. That's what counts."

Wait a minute. Did I miss something? "Larry, you know it's been almost three years since we've been together..."

"And you're wondering if I been fucking other women. Right? Well, yeah. I have. I was an unattached, healthy, heterosexual male over the age of consent. Damn right I been busy! But I've been careful. I'm clean."

"No. That's not what I was going to say. I'm kinda surprised that you just took it for granted that we're back together. I mean we haven't spoken in almost three years."

"You said you need me. My feelings for you haven't changed. You're the only one for me. All the others were just something to past the time. They knew it."

"What if I hadn't come back?"

"But you did."

"Don't you care if I've been faithful to you?"

"Oh, I care if there've been other men in your life. I care a good goddam! But I can't do anything about what happened when we weren't together."

He signaled the waitress for the check. "C'mon back to my place. I have something for you."

We walked the three blocks to Larry's apartment in silence. Nostalgia crept in as we passed familiar places along the way: Rose's Garden, where he always bought me the most beautiful flowers for no reason at all; Inkwell, where he got my initials tattooed on his groin; Redbox, where we rented DVDs we never watched all the way through the first time.

By the time we reached Larry's apartment I was beginning to rethink my plan. Walking into the living room did nothing for my state of confusion. The room was filled with brightly wrapped packages of all shapes and sizes. Valentine's Day, Christmas, Easter, Sweetest Day and my birthday all were represented. Closer inspection revealed gifts for Fat Tuesday, Independence Day, Memorial Day, Thanksgiving, New Year's Day, President's Day, Halloween. There was even a box with a handmade card wishing me a Happy Ground Hog Day. *Who celebrates Ground Hog Day?*

"What's all of this?"

"All the gifts I bought for you over the last thirty-one months, six days and two hours."

This was not going according to plan. "You just can't treat me this way!" I screamed.

"What's wrong with the way I treat you? I never cheated when we were together. I remember to put the seat down. I never forget your birthday. Or any holiday they make cards for. I always open doors for you. Never once have I expected you to foot the bill – not even half of it. And I always make sure you come before me. What more could you want?"

I suppose that's a laundry list some women dream of, but it wasn't mine.

"The problem is I love you," I said. As contrary as it was to everything I consciously believed in, I loved Larry Freeman. Larry Freeman who was a throwback to another generation. Larry Freeman who believed that the sexes aren't and never could be equal. Larry Freeman who was by word and action a womanizing bastard. That was the problem. Well the heart was not gonna get what it wanted this time!

"I love you, too. Why is that a problem?"

"Because you're...you!" I was visibly shaking.

Why was he trying to make it so simple? I let out a guttural scream, took out my gun, aimed at the largest package in the room and pulled the trigger. Even though the gun shot a blank from the chamber, the force was enough to rip through the package and get my point across.

"What..."

Before he could finish the thought, I aimed at his manhood and pulled the trigger.

For one measurable moment, the world stopped. There was no explosive fire flash following the click this time. I was no fool. I had left the clip empty.

Larry closed the distance between us, and tried to take me in his arms.

"The only reason you're alive is that it's illegal to kill even the likes of you. Now stay the fuck out of my life!"

"You're a crazy bitch!" Larry called after me, as I walked towards the door.

"Yeah, but I'm not your crazy bitch any longer."

The door was closed between us now. I leaned back against it, and for the first time in a long time I could breathe. I had achieved closure, and a mind-bending orgasm in the process.

~ニ~ニ~ニ~ニ~ニ~ニ~

It's been a year since that explosive confrontation with Larry. I've learned a lot about myself and why I was so crazy when it came to our relationship. It was all about control and perception and expectation. I thought I was losing control; I thought Larry was taking it away. As it turned out, I was just plain scared of true love with its warts and all.

I have matured enough to know that perfect love is a lie created by marketing gurus, and that love shouldn't be synthesized into a saccharine facsimile of reality. I realize that knowing oneself, and standing firm in that knowledge, does not make one an egomaniac.

Now, on my dad's arm, walking down the aisle to publicly pledge my love to one man, who loves me unconditionally, I can honestly say that the demon is dead.

Dad gives my hand to my groom, and I am elated as his fingers entwine with mine. I know that no other woman will ever see my initials tattooed in his groin, that he will cherish and take care of me, as I have learned to honor and care for him, that he will always bring me flowers and celebrate the silliest of holidays with me. For as long as we both shall live.

Afterword

It's been several weeks since I read *Passages* from cover to cover again. I see elements in these stories that are dear to me: love, family, friendship, purpose. Some of the vignettes may be a bit unorthodox, but those elements still shine through.

In hindsight, I recognize that this book has been a passage for me, as well. I have stepped from the introspective state of writer into the critical world of published author. It has required a little sister's steadfastness, Candi's faith and Kitty's trust. And a village of support.

Thank you for purchasing *Passages* and being part of that village.

And now, I'm dying to know... was there a story that resonated with you; was there a character you'd like to hear more from? Perhaps you can inspire me to continue their story.

I'd love to hear your thoughts, and look forward to our next literary meet-up.

passagesfeedback@ameritech.net

About the Author

Jo McEntee is a native of Chicago, Illinois. She curates the weekly Writers Workshop at Stony Island Arts Bank, teaches computer technology to seniors at Harry S. Truman College, and creates docent-led experiences at Smart Museum of Art.

Made in the USA
San Bernardino, CA
16 October 2018